THE LODGER OVERHEAD
AND OTHERS

Blackwood was standing entirely on his own feet.

THE
LODGER OVERHEAD
AND OTHERS

BY
CHARLES BELMONT DAVIS

ILLUSTRATED

Short Story Index Reprint Series

 BOOKS FOR LIBRARIES PRESS
FREEPORT, NEW YORK

First Published 1909
Reprinted 1970

STANDARD BOOK NUMBER:
8369-3489-X

LIBRARY OF CONGRESS CATALOG CARD NUMBER:
71-121533

PRINTED IN THE UNITED STATES OF AMERICA

To
N. D.

CONTENTS

ILLUSTRATIONS

THE LODGER OVERHEAD

THE LODGER OVERHEAD

THE thought has occurred to me of late, with such frequency and with so much insistence, that I am strongly inclined to believe that it must have always lain dormant somewhere in one of the cells of my brain. As a child, and later as a young man, I enjoyed the same moderate exhilaration which all city-bred folk seem to feel for the clean air, the blue sky, the flowered fields, and the sheltering forests of the country; but according to this theory, of late so constantly before me, I can not but well believe that the original intention of Fate was that I should live my little span of years on a well-watered, well-wooded farm; that such a mind as had been allotted to me should ripen under broad skies and a blazing sun; that my body should grow strong in the open fields; that the horse munching his oats in his stall, the fat pink pig in his sty, the chickens and geese and the turkeys in the farmyard, I should count among my intimates. Just as sure as I am that I should have broadened in the pure air and developed on the simple product of the farm, just so sure am I that under the same benign influences I should have mellowed in soul and body and some of these days withered away in the twilight, as it fell over the fields and gradually darkened into the purple night. But things do not always happen as they were intended. Just as Fate was about to leave me in peace at a nice old farmhouse somebody seems to have nudged Fate's elbow, and I was inadvertently dropped into a three-room bachelor flat on a side street between Broadway and Fifth Avenue, although I must confess that my immediate neighborhood is more redolent of the former thoroughfare—the moral tone of the little street improving greatly as it approaches the more aristocratic avenue.

Below me, on the street floor, there is a shop where guests from the nearby hotels and many ladies of the stage have their soiled gloves and lingerie shirt-waists cleaned, and just over this is a more ornately decorated floor where Madame Quelquechose sells Paris hats and manteaux to a most exclusive carriage

4

THE LODGER OVERHEAD

trade. Above me there is one more three-room apartment, very much like my own, occupied at various
times by various neighbors (names unknown) who
glower at me and then hurry on through the ill-lit
hallways. Across the street, just opposite, there is the
stage-door of a theatre much given over to comic
operas, and in front of this there is an iron railing
enclosing a small yard where the surly doorkeeper sits
all the day and most of the night playing with a black
cat; and here it is that the chorus girls linger for a
last word with the men friends who modestly accompany them afoot or more ostentatiously whirl them
up in dark, silent hansoms or in glistening, noisy,
brass-bound automobiles.

At the Fifth Avenue end of the street there is a
most stately looking and somewhat old-fashioned
apartment house; next to this two fine examples of
the old-time New York homes still occupied by de-
scendants of the original Dutch families who built
them. Both sides of the street are faced with shops
much like those under my own modest home, and
above these there are many hives for men and women
bachelors. Of my neighbors I know, or the world at

5

large knows, but little—the blinds are down and the curtains drawn except on such occasions as when a fire-engine clangs by or a parade with a blaring band passes along Fifth Avenue.

So far as I can judge, most of us on this particular side street, always excepting those at the two homes of the aristocrats, lead pretty much the same kind of life—that is, so far as our meals are concerned. For breakfast we depend on our "visiting valets" and colored maids, and for luncheon and dinner we go to the Hofbrauhaus or to the restaurant around the corner on Broadway. Of course, there are many and brilliant exceptions to this régime; quite frequently at night a grande dame, usually accompanied by a *jeune fille*, from one of the two exclusive homes, drives away in the family coach, and hardly a night passes that a hansom or a glistening brougham does not dash around the corner at our end of the street and stop before one or another of the dark, fore-boding, brownstone fronts. A young man, in evening clothes, jumps lightly out, throws away his cigarette, and disappears in the dark vestibule at the top of the brownstone steps; but we all continue to peek

6

out from behind our green holland shades, for we know that the best part is yet to come. Sometimes she keeps us waiting a long time, but it is well worth the while, for she is always looking quite lovely in her diaphanous filmy clothes and a lace coat and a big hat (generally black), a mass of golden trinkets at her waist and a square gold purse swinging from her white-gloved hand. As they pass we can see the glow of the girl's dress and the man's broad shirt front and the little red light from his cigarette. It is not difficult for us less fortunate ones to imagine that we can even detect the smiling features of the callow youth and hear the low laughter of the girl, for we know that they are off to the gay world of red lamp-shades and Hungarian bands, of vintage wines and the very best of French cooking.

Of the many lodgers who have occupied the rooms over my own I can not recall any one who was the immediate cause of hansoms or highly burnished broughams blocking our thoroughfare. Of the personality of these various lodgers, I have, as a rule, been wholly ignorant. At intervals I have met them on the stairway; once there was a little child who played about the hallways in a lonely sort of way and with whom I exchanged greetings, but for the most part my acquaintance has extended no further than a passing glance at the new and unknown name over the letter-box next to my own, and the occasional sound of anonymous footfalls overhead.

I was a little surprised—not a little annoyed, too —one afternoon, to have my nap interrupted by a sharp rapping at my bedroom door. Although rather inadequately clad, I opened the door and saw a messenger boy standing in the dimly lit hallway. With one hand he offered me a telegram and with the other the book which he wished me to sign. The light was bad, and my eyes were still heavy with sleep, and, at the first glance, I failed to see my name on the soiled page at which the record was opened.

"Sign it yourself," I said in a most peevish manner, and, taking the telegram from him, I slammed the door in his face.

Still calling down curses on the correspondent who had so thoughtlessly interrupted my nap, I switched on the light and glanced at the writing on the envelope. The name was that of a woman, and one

8

which I had never met with before. I hurriedly opened the door and called down the stairway; but the messenger had disappeared.

As the name on the telegram was not that of either of the occupants of the two shops below me, I at once reached the logical conclusion that it must be that of my unknown neighbor overhead. Without more ado, I got into my bathroom slippers, pulled on a long overcoat, and started up the stairway leading to the apartment above.

In answer to my knock the door was opened by a young girl, and, in the subdued light of the room back of her, it seemed to me the brilliancy of her beauty was quite spectacular and almost too wonderful to be of this workaday world. In any case, I know that the drowsiness from which I had been suffering left me as suddenly and as completely as if I had been thrust into a cold plunge.

The girl's costume it is not easy for me to describe, but, apparently, it consisted of yards of filmy lace, with many blue bows sewn on it, and endless narrow blue ribbons running through it. On the whole, so far as quantity went, with the exception of

9

the bare arms and throat, she was fairly well concealed. Barring the strip of bare ankles, showing
between the bottom of my overcoat and my bath
slippers, I might safely make the same claim for my
own appearance. The girl was quite without em-
barrassment, and for a moment stood at the door
smiling at my confusion.

"Won't you come in?" she said at last, and I followed her to the centre of the room.

My neighbor was undoubtedly an artist, and I had
evidently stumbled into her workshop. Through a
dim orange light I noted that the tinted walls were
partially draped with pieces of tapestry; ornately
embroidered copes and stoles from the Italian
churches of the early part of the last century were
thrown over the backs of some splendid pieces of
old furniture, and many half-finished sketches and
unframed portraits stood about on easels and against
the walls in great confusion. I must confess that the
condition of the room did not speak well for my
neighbor in her capacity of housekeeper. The pictures, the draperies, the furniture—even the floor—
were covered with a thick layer of dust, which appa-

rently had been allowed to accumulate for weeks, and was in the most extraordinary contrast to the spiritual, almost eery, beauty of the girl and the glistening freshness of her voluminous lace petticoats.

"I am very sorry to disturb you," I said, "but I have brought you a telegram, which was left me by mistake. You must pardon my dress, or rather the lack of it, but the messenger interrupted my forty-winks."

"Forty-winks?" she repeated, and shrugged her pretty shoulders. "That's what it used to be a long time ago, but now it is fairly an orgie of sleep. You can not deny that, when you were young, an alarm clock sufficed, but to-day it is necessary for your man to wake you in time for your dinner hour."

My unknown neighbor looked at me with a curious little wistful smile, as if she were quite out of humor with my bachelor ways; sighed, crossed the room to where a high lamp stood, looked at the address on the telegram, and then carefully tore off the end of the envelope. She stood under the broad orange lamp-shade, her small, piquant face, with its deep, warm coloring, half-turned toward me; the soft golden light fell full on a great mass of wavy bronze hair, the well-rounded throat, and the wonderfully pink-and-white arms. I could not help wondering if I should ever see them again. In all ways she was the embodiment of youth and health and condition, and yet the very brilliancy of her beauty seemed to surround her with a certain glow which set her apart from the ordinary human being, and I was immensely impressed, too, by the fact, both at the time and afterward, that when she walked the soles of her tiny Turkish slippers left no mark on the dusty floor.

When the girl had finished reading the telegram, she put it back into its envelope and held it toward me.

"This is not for me," she said.

"Then why did you read it?" I gasped, out of pure surprise.

"Because I wanted to know what was in it."

"Do you consider it your right to know everything that is in every telegram or letter?" I asked. "I should think your curiosity might lead you into considerable trouble."

She smiled at me pleasantly enough, but it was the kind of smile that a mother might vouchsafe her wayward child.

"My interest," she said, "extends no farther than Our Street. That is my province."

"If that is your province, then," I said, "where may I find the lady to whom this is addressed?"

"She is a *vendeuse* in the hat-shop of Madame Quelquechose, on the second floor."

I bowed my thanks, and, as there seemed no further excuse for me to remain, I started toward the door, when I conceived what at the time I considered a splendid idea and a subtle piece of detective work.

"Will you not write 'opened by mistake' on this?" I asked, "and sign your name?"

Again she looked at me with the same sweet, superior smile, and, with a knowing look in her big eyes, slowly shook her head.

"I'm so sorry," she said. "You know you were really very kind to bring me the telegram. Good-by."

"Good-by," I repeated, "seems hardly neighborly. Might it not rather be *au revoir?*"

"No," she said, smiling, "I fear it might not.

13

Neighbors are, after all, but a question of geography, and the result of a certain sameness of income. An enforced meeting over a stray telegram can hardly be said to constitute an introduction."

For the first time the tone of indifference, the almost severity of her language, brought to me a painful consciousness of my bare ankles and my otherwise somewhat informal garb, and I clumsily began to back toward the door.

"Oh, very well," I said, assuming a manner as flippant as I could well master under the circumstances, "if you prefer it that way—our happy meeting will be just as if it never was."

She slightly inclined her pretty head. "Just as if it never was," she repeated.

When I reached the door I bowed low, trying my best to be gracious and, at the same time, to conceal my bare ankles. "I can only trust, then," I added as a parting word, "that fate will be so kind as to throw us once more together in our very narrow hallway."

I was well on my way down the stairway when I felt conscious of the girl having followed me to her doorway. As I turned she leaned over the banister and whispered: "And you needn't look for my name on the letter-box in the hall; it isn't there, really. Good-by."

I returned to my room, where I found my evening paper waiting for me, and, although I learned on the very first page that one near friend had been thrown from his automobile and another had had his head cracked open at polo, I could not switch my thoughts from the young woman overhead. Here was sufficient youth and loveliness to make the front page of any newspaper seem dull enough, and I confess that her indifference, which might have been construed by the more fastidious as crass rudeness, annoyed me a good deal. Before my paper was half finished, I threw it aside and, hurriedly finishing my dressing, went down to the vestibule on the lower floor. She was quite right; the little brass letter-box next my own bore the name of a man, and, judging from the fact that it was stuffed full of advertisements of new cheap restaurants and "home" laundries, it had evidently not been used for a long time. As soon as I reached my office the following morning I called up the agent from whom I rented my apartment. The agent was a personal friend—by disposition, a cotillion leader, but by inheritance the owner and agent of many houses, of which mine was one.

"Pardon me, Grayson," I said, as soon as I could get him to the telephone, "but I believe that I have been a pretty good tenant, have paid my rent the first day of every month, and have never complained about my neighbors."

"You are in all things," Grayson drawled, "the perfect tenant."

"Good!" said I. "Now, after fifteen years, I am going to ask you a favor."

"Is it a plumber or the man with the white enamel paint? It's always one or the other with you tenants."

"Neither," said I, "but I want to know all that you know about the beautiful young person that lives in the apartment over mine?"

"Nothing at all, personally," said Grayson; "but I'll ask somebody in the office here."

There was a few moments' delay, broken by the rumblings of an indistinguishable conversation through the telephone, and then Grayson began again:

"That apartment was rented to an artist chap named Hoffmeyer for six months on an unexpired lease. He said that, as he was often away from town for quite a long while, painting portraits, he would pay in advance, which he did. That's all I know."

"Do you suppose the beautiful person is Mrs. Hoffmeyer?" I asked.

"How should I know?" said Grayson. "Why don't you run upstairs and ask her yourself?"

"Are you aware," I continued, somewhat aggrieved at his ignorance and indifference, "that the platform of the fire-escape on that top floor extends to the buildings on either side, and, if the rear windows should be left unlatched, any one could enter the back room of the apartment either from the fire-escape or even the roof?"

"To you who live there," said Grayson, with a most aggravating nasal inflection, "I have no doubt that those are most illuminating and stirring facts, but to a commuter from Irvington, like myself, believe me, they are wholly without interest. I know

nor care nothing about your beautiful neighbor.
However, in a general way, I would take a commuter's advice—'Stop, look, listen!'"

I have said that I did not know my neighbors,
which is quite true, but I did know something about
one of them, who happened to live almost directly
across the street from me. She was employed as a
stenographer downtown during the day and eked out
rather a miserable existence by making neckties for
a very limited trade at night. That afternoon I
watched for her until I saw her enter the house opposite, and a few minutes later open one of the
windows of her apartment. I hurried over and was
at once admitted to her little sitting-room, which
looked out over the street. I told her the ostensible
object of my visit and the name of the client who
had recommended her.

With a show of much pleasure she brought out a
great variety of silk stuffs from which the ties were
to be made. Pleading a lack of light with which to
see the colors, I looked at the windows of the apartment over my own, and saw that they were not only
closed and the shades down, but apparently the

18

window-sills and the windows themselves were gray with dirt and dust.

"I live directly opposite," I said, "in Number Fourteen. Apparently my neighbor in the apartment over my own is away. One must cross the street to really learn what is going on in one's own house."

"I never thought of that," said Miss Dawson, "but I believe I do know more about my neighbors across the street than of my own fellow lodgers. You must be quite alone at night now in your building—those windows have not been opened for a long time?"

"You are sure!" I asked.

"Oh, yes," she said, "I am quite sure, because a German-looking young man used to sit there every afternoon smoking a pipe just about this time. I quite miss him."

"I don't think I ever saw him," I said. "He had a wife, I believe?"

The girl shook her head. "Perhaps—but I never saw her. I rather imagined he was alone. A colored girl used to look after the apartment and cook for him, I think."

19

THE LODGER OVERHEAD

I chose the silk for several ties, and, having given my order, bade Miss Dawson good-night. It was quite evident that I could learn but little of the beautiful lady overhead from my neighbors across the street, and it was equally apparent that, for one reason or another, she chose to confine her operations to the rear of the apartment. For the next few days my ears were forever listening for a noise of any kind from overhead, but I could hear nothing. The girl seemed to neither come nor go, at least by the staircase; her letter-box remained stuffed with circulars, and the window-sills of her front windows begrimed in dust. If she left or entered the house, at least while I was in it, then I was convinced that she did so by way of the fire-escape in the rear.

The days and nights passed on, and as I heard or saw nothing of her, I admit that I became restless, peevish with my friends, and very ill at ease. There were times when a glance and a few words from a pretty neighbor would have passed almost unnoticed, and have been at once overwhelmed in the swirl of other things. But there was not so much of a swirl to my life these days—it was much more orderly and more carefully regulated in every way, and not nearly so full of incident or adventure. I now preferred a quiet dinner at my club to the noise and gaiety of the restaurants; and whereas I had formerly been a most persistent theatregoer, at present I found it difficult to sit through any play, however worthy. Formal calls and parties I had given up entirely, and the women I had grown up with and knew really well, I found just a little old and a little too devoted to home interests and to their daughters' social successes. Of course, as the mothers were a little too old, the daughters themselves were just a little too young; so there I was, a human pendulum swinging between the two generations—and the pendulum swinging a little more slowly every year.

It was, perhaps, a week after my interview with my neighbor when I saw her again. I had returned from a supper party after the play, and, although it was late, I picked up a book and, dropping into an easy chair, prepared for an hour's quiet reading before going to bed. I had barely become really interested

THE LODGER OVERHEAD

when I heard the door of the apartment overhead close, and, a few moments later, a creak from the shaky banisters told me that some one was coming downstairs. As noiselessly as possible I stole across my sitting-room, and, pulling aside the silk curtain a very little, peeped out through the glass in the door leading to the hall. I saw the girl cautiously tiptoeing her way down the stairs. She was apparently dressed very much as I had seen her before, but her volumi-nous and beribboned petticoats were partially con-cealed by a wonderful pink affair of lace and diaph-anous silk—a most extraordinary garment, I thought, for a young woman to choose for street wear at one o'clock in the morning. She wore no hat or head-covering of any kind, but the bronze-colored hair had apparently been arranged with the greatest possible care. Even in the dim light of the hall she appeared most lovely, and from my hiding-place I watched her until she disappeared down the staircase leading to the shops and the street. The front door is a heavy one, with a stiff lock, and it is impossible to open and shut it without making a considerable noise. I stood in the centre of my room, waiting for some moments, but, hearing no noise of any kind, I opened my door and walked down the hallway to the head of the stairs. They were quite deserted, but a shaft of strong white light fell across the hall-way from the open door of the shop of Madame Quelquechose. I cautiously stole down the steps and gently knocked on the door-frame.

"Come in," said the voice of my neighbor from the far end of the shop. It was a long, narrow room, the walls covered with pink brocade, and at regular distances there were white-and-gold showcases, with long mirrored doors; the floor was carpeted in dark green, and standing about in carefully arrayed con-fusion were a number of gilded, spindle-legged chairs and many tall, delicately stemmed stands, topped by gorgeously flowered and beribboned hats. The girl had already opened several of the show-cases, and I saw bewildering rows of lace coats and cloth wraps of many delicate shades. My neighbor was standing before a mirror; a heavy lace coat fell from her shoulders, and she was carefully placing on her well-poised head a broad, black hat with a great bow of dark green velvet on the side.

"Do you like it?" she asked, softly patting the bronze curls over her forehead.

"Beautiful!" said I. "How did you get in?"

"It's very simple. When Madame Quelquechose stays late at night, she leaves the key under the door-mat, so that the boy can open the shop in the morning. It is perfectly safe except from you and me. I stumbled over the key quite by accident."

I carefully removed several marvellously plumed hats from one of the spindle-legged chairs and sat down. "Do you come here often of nights?" I asked.

The girl surveyed herself critically in the glass, and pushed the hat forward over her forehead and the bronze curls. "Quite often," she said. "It's rather an amusing game. You see I play I'm different people on Our Street."

"Splendid!" I said. "Who do you think you are now?"

She glanced in the mirror at the reflection of the spreading hat, with its dash of brilliant color, and then down at the loosely hanging lace coat, reaching almost to her patent-leather slippers.

"Who do I think I am now?" she repeated.

"Now I am the Bachelor Girl across the street—hardly the person you would introduce to your mother—although, perhaps, you might to your sister. Respectable, maybe, but, after all, I am a little young and a trifle pretty, perhaps, to live alone; and, when a girl does that with a family in Harlem, the neighbors *will* talk. And then I constantly dine with men alone"—the girl turned and shook her pretty head at me, but the smile that played about her red lips seemed just a trifle knowing and rather worldly—"but you can't blame me, can you? Ever since father lost his fortune in a wheat deal, the flat uptown is so terribly dull—and I do like a good dinner after sitting about all day really doing nothing. And then it isn't as if I didn't call on my people every few days and spend a month during the summer with them—is it?" She sighed at her own filial devotion.

"Do you suppose the people on Our Street," I asked, "know just when you are starting out to visit your folks and just when you are off to a matinée?"

"I wonder," she said, with a slight contraction of

her delicate eyebrows, "I wonder. But I do so love these occasional dips into Bohemia."

"The threads which draw you back to the shores of comparative respectability after these dips," I suggested, "are, in reality, but slight. Be careful they don't snap some day, and leave you floundering about and calling for help."

The girl smiled most cheerfully. "I could get help all right in Bohemia. It's being left to flounder on the shores of the dead sea of respectability that I fear. They so love to see one of their own gasping for life on the hot sands."

"Well enough for the present," I said, "but how about the future? Now you have health and beauty and the capacity of youth for pleasure, but that won't last always. Some day the shadows and the crow's-feet and the creases will come, and the young men will stay away—that is, if they haven't already married young women who live with their folks. For some reason young men seem to prefer young women for wives who live with their folks—no?"

The girl made a little grimace at me by way of the mirror, and swung herself about so that she could better see the hang of her lace coat in the back. "Perhaps," she said, "but, you see, I've really had no experience. Now, you're awfully old, and you no doubt have watched the people of Our Street grow up, and it has made you sour and discontented and cynical. You forget the day you came to Our Street. I wager you you had no thought of crow's-feet and wrinkles then. I doubt if you knew a natural complexion from rouge, or even enamel, in those days."

"Quite right, my dear," I said—and the fact that I said "my dear" was admission enough that her suppositions were perfectly correct—"I came here twenty years ago, and every woman was beautiful then, and every complexion was the work of God. But now!" I threw up my hands in mock horror.

She turned and looked down on me, wide-eyed, and slowly shook her head. "Twenty years on a side street in New York!" she said. "What a life—what a life! You are, of course, the oldest inhabitant, and your constitution must be a marvellous affair to have kept you going all that time. You should have crawled off to die in your native town long before this. A refuge for reclaimed women or an inebriates' home should have had your name carved over its doors years ago. Just think of your spending your own money for twenty years—it's shocking! Don't you really feel like dying? I should think that your aches and pains would be quite unbearable."

I slowly stuck my legs out before me and stretched my arms above my head. "You see," I said, "I am still quite strong. I admit that I am somewhat more temperate in my habits, and now that you mention the fact that I am awfully old, I don't mind confessing that I have been thinking a great deal of late of moving to a home in the country."

The girl turned sharply from the mirror to which she had returned and looked down at me, as if to satisfy herself that I was quite serious. Finding that I was, she broke into such loud and merry peals of laughter that the broad hat wabbled on her head until it was necessary to hold it on with both hands.

"You," she said, with real tears of laughter glistening in her eyes—"a country squire! You would die of ennui in a week!"

THE LODGER OVERHEAD

I admit that her laughter annoyed me, although I confess her youthful beauty more than made up for this, for it seemed to radiate the more brilliantly every new moment that I was near her.

"You don't understand," I said with considerable asperity. "You're only a child and can't appreciate the beauties of nature—the passion of the middle-aged for the blossoming flower of the fields and the love we feel for the shadows in a crystal stream."

She ceased her laughter and sat down on a chair facing my own and interlaced her long pink fingers behind the back of her pretty head.

"Don't lose your sense of humor," she said—"blossoming plants and crystal streams, fiddlesticks! Of course *I* can appreciate the beauties of nature. I could leave all this to-morrow and never come back. I could live on milk and honey and dream away my life under an apple tree, with only the birds and insects for my friends, but I am young and still sensitive to many beautiful things; my pulse is fresh and strong and my lungs are yet free from the tainted air of your great city. Should you, for instance, draw a breath of perfectly good air into your lungs, you would probably collapse entirely. And if you didn't, you would grope your way back to this—and—and —rejuvenate. My dear, good old man——"

"I am just turned forty," I interrupted.

"My dear, good old man," she continued, "you may dream of blossoming plants and crystal streams, but the poison of the town is in your veins. A man who has driven a racing car over oiled roads never returns to a top buggy. The rooms overhead, believe me, will know you until the end."

"Knowing this," I said, "and with your lungs and your heart, no doubt, still so pure, why do you not go at once to your apple tree and your birds and your insects?"

"Why?" she asked. "Because the power to go is still mine. I am just looking in at the door of Our Street, and I confess that it looks warm and comfortable enough. I am like one of my insect friends if you will, fluttering in a circle about the flame you love so well, but the circle is yet a large one, my wings are still intact, and I can fly away should I so will it. Besides, all the women on Our Street do not wear lace coats." She put aside the broad hat and

30

the long coat and, going over to the mirrored case, took down a white cloth cape, exquisite in its simplicity, and drew it closely about her slim figure.

"And now?" I asked.

"Now, I am the Jeune Fille at the end of the street"—at the moment it seemed to me that her whole expression had softened materially, and there was a timid, almost shy, look in the big eyes. "Poor, if you will," she continued, "and left behind; ashamed of my address, but always proud of my name. My chances are dimmed, of course, by the daughters of the trust kings from the Middle West, but I have still a few relatives who live about Washington Square and a few others scattered along the right side of the park. They gave me teas when I first came out and now they ask me to their large dances in winter and their country places in the summer. And I am always carefully chaperoned."

"And you get money presents at Christmas?" I suggested, "and your rich relatives speak of your poverty as if it were inherited tuberculosis."

The girl sighed, but went back to the mirror, and with a smile of pleasure noted how charming her piquant face looked peeping out from the high braided collar of the white cloth mantle.

"It's an awful struggle, I know," she sighed, nodding her head at the face in the mirror. "to be so wise in the ways of the world and yet to look on at it all with innocent, meaningless eyes, and then, dear mother is so difficult. She can not understand why money should rank above beauty and pure worth, and why the price of eggs and butter goes up while the morals of the young men go down. She insists that I marry an old man like yourself, whose securities have withstood the panics of twenty years, and whose wild oats have been garnered long ago and forgotten under the dust of the law of limitations."

"A horrible alternative," I said, turning just far enough to see myself in the mirror of a neighborly show-case. "And yet my hair is not even gray. I admit that I have recently regarded marriage as a remote possibility, but——"

"A remote possibility!" she echoed. "A man so set in his ways! You're really too absurd. Why, I'm sure you have your bath drawn and your coffee served within five minutes of the same hour every morning of the year. You should apply to the nearest hospital for a trained nurse, not at one of our oldest homes for a child-wife."

"You're very discouraging " I said. "You forget that a bachelor's passion for a quiet married life is dearer to him than anything, except his love of freedom. Can't you play you are somebody else?"

"Surely," the girl answered, in a most flippant manner. She threw the chaste white cape over the nearest chair, and, returning to the show-case, took down a most bewildering affair, which, with a proper spirit of awe, I draped about her white shoulders. It was a wrap of great intrinsic worth and of superlative beauty, all of gold-spangled net, over rose-colored chiffon, with very large ruffled sleeves and an immense fichu of chiffon and lace. From one of the stands she took a broad felt hat with a heavy binding and drooping plumes, all of the most exquisite shade of domingo pink, and, going back to the mirror, placed it with much care over the mass of bronze curls. With her hands on her hips, she

33

turned and twisted before the pier-glass, until she was, to all appearances, quite satisfied that the girl and the hat and the wrap were a combination of nature and artifice at its very best. With a broad sweep of the mantle, a riot of gorgeous color bewildering in its very audacity, she took a few steps toward the chair to which I had returned, and courtesied low before me. There was no further any attempt to conceal the knowledge in her soul. It shone brazenly now through the big meaning eyes, and about the arched lips there was the suggestion of a most knowing smile.

"Charming," I said, "quite charming!" and I drew my coat over my broad shirt-bosom as if her very presence chilled me. "But what a wicked, cruel little smile. Whom does *it* belong to?"

"My idea," she said, looking at herself in the mirror with the most frank smile of adulation over her own beauty, "was to be fascinating rather than cruel. It pleases me to think that I am the Show Girl who has sublet the apartment from the girl in Number Forty-two, the one who has gone on the road with 'The Maid and the Mandarin.'"

"A show girl," I mused aloud. "Personally, I do not like the type. I have often seen you trail the balayeuse of your silken skirts across the pavement on your way to and from your electric cab, but so far you have been a stranger to me. I have even been urged to attend your supper parties, and each time I have refused. So you see, my young friend, there is one crime on the calendar of Our Street of which I am still innocent."

"Still innocent!" she laughed at me, and I hated her, for her laughter seemed so very hard and had a metallic ring. "Still innocent! Quite right. I am a bird of plumage, whose brilliancy dazzles only the untrained eye of the very young or the fading sight of the very old. Soggy, middle-aged respectability knows me for what I am, a mummy dressed by Paquin. Escaped me in your youth perhaps you have, but, after all, that is long since, and I am a product of the present century. But, I wager you, the swish of these silken skirts will yet be music to your faded hearing, and some day, believe me, you will be a willing and an honored guest at my supper table."

35

"As well say," I protested, "that I will ask the very pretty *vendeuse* who is forever leaning against the door-frame of Number Forty-two to dine at Sherry's, or that I will put up at my club the haberdasher's clerk across the way."

"Pardon me," said the girl haughtily, tilting her dimpled chin in the most charming fashion, and as if my last remark had given serious offence. "You are quite wrong to mix the social and commercial life of Our Street. The *Vendeuse* and the Haberdasher's Clerk, however worthy, have not even the status of the Extra Girl and the Chorus Man who use the stage-door opposite; or of Carlo the bootblack, who knows the inside story of every pair of shoes on the block; or even of the Telephone Girl at the corner drug-store, who can ring any of us up without looking in the book. Believe me, the persons you mentioned have no standing whatever—and Heaven forbid that they should have any effect on our life. They are but transients, at best, and have no more intercourse with the people of Our Street than they do with the casual shoppers from Broadway or Fifth Avenue."

She really seemed to have forgotten me entirely.

"I like that," I said. "Do you consider yourself one of us just because you have subleased an apartment for a few months?" In some nook or corner of the shop my beautiful neighbor had discovered a curtain-rod painted white, and, using it as a staff, such as the ladies affected at the time of the Empire, she proceeded to parade slowly up and down in front of the row of mirrors, and smile and bow with much condescension at her reflections, just as if she were greeting her lady friends in some royal gardens. She really seemed to have forgotten me entirely, and I found it necessary to repeat my remark.

"Because you have rented an apartment in the neighborhood," I said, "during the short run in New York of the company of which you are a member, does that make you one of us?"

"It makes no difference," she said slowly, stalking with a great manner up and down before the mirrors, "whether I or another show girl occupies the room. The character of the tenants never varies on Our Street. The girl who sublet her apartments to me used the same sachet powder in the bureau drawers as I do, and the same violet ammonia tablets for her bath—the scent was unmistakable in both cases. Should your ghost dare the natural hazards of Our Street and return here after your demise, it would find another bachelor ensconced and very much like yourself. There would be a different brand of Scotch on the sideboard, perhaps, and a new face on the bureau-top, surely, but the general effect would be quite the same."

"You are terribly cynical for one so young," I said. "Do you even consider yourself a fair example of your type? Do you really for one moment think yourself typical of a kind of neighbor with whom I must one day be neighborly? Even if flowered fields and running brooks are not for me, surely do not tell me that one day I must kneel to you and your cape of gold. Because I have tasted sherry in my youth, must I turn to brandy in my old age? If, from mere exhaustion, a man drops out of the rush of a great city, is it necessary to look on such beauty as yours before he can return to action?"

The girl stopped in front of a mirror, and, drawing herself to her full height, grasped her staff in both hands and looked steadfastly into the glass, as if she were posing for a portrait by some great master. Then, in answer to my question, she slightly inclined her head toward the image in the glass.

"I am typical of my class, and I am typical of the pleasures of your city. I am for show, and I dine with the one who considers it most worth his while to pay for my presence—the pleasure of dining opposite so much beauty and such fine clothes. It is only a question of time when most of you come to paying for your pleasures—you love your restaurants better than your own dining-rooms, and your theatres better than your libraries. Believe me, yours is the city of boughten happiness. You ask me if I am typical of my class. I am no more typical of my class than you are of yours—no more typical than Carlo the bootblack, or the Girl Who Makes Silk Ties for extra money with which to buy theatre tickets, or the Jeune Fille who is stranded at the end of the block, or the Bachelor Maid across the way who doesn't live with her folks, or the Decayed Gentlewoman who runs the lingerie shop at Number Twenty-two, or the Telephone Girl at the corner drug-store, or the other denizens of the side streets, who, behind drawn shades, watch the life of the city rush on through its great thoroughfares. Do any of us of the side street ever run for public office or corner a wheat deal and become famous in a night, or do any of us fail and hang out the red flag of the auctioneer? Not we—we take the middle course and live on the safe, easy banks of the stream, and watch the ebb and flow of the tide—and wait."

The girl laid aside her improvised wand, took off the plumed hat, and hung the spangled wrap in the mirrored case. Together we rearranged the shop as we had found it, locked the door, and hid the key under the mat. Slowly I followed her up to the landing before my door. With one step on the stairway leading to the floor above, she stopped and held out her hand to me.

"Good-by!" she said, "and for the last time."

"Surely not that?" I urged. "I don't even know your name."

"My name," she said; "my name is Youth."

"Youth?" I repeated.

"Youth, if you will. I am the spirit of the cross-town streets—I am the writing on the wall—I am the

40

"Good-by, old man," she whispered; "good-by!"

THE LODGER OVERHEAD

grist ready for the mill—you are the chaff ready for the winds."

She started up the stairs, but after she had taken a few steps, turned, and, with the same wistful smile that I had loved so much, looked back at me over her shoulder.

"Good-by, old man," she whispered; "good-by!"

"Good-by! Youth," I said. "We've had some good times together, you and I. Here's God-speed to you, whichever path you choose!"

The girl smiled back at me, hesitated for a moment, and then with no more words ran lightly up the steps, and I heard the door close sharply behind her.

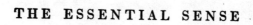

THE ESSENTIAL SENSE

THE ESSENTIAL SENSE

I

IN leaving the hotel porch after nightfall they had broken the oldest and most sacred tradition of the Leesburg Springs. The suggestion had come from Amy Burden as she sat with her *fiancé* in the blackest corner of the hotel piazza, and this piazza was noted throughout the South for its particularly black corners. The idea was conceived in a certain distrust of her lover's sporting blood, but it must be said, to the young man's credit, that if he winced at the proposition his chagrin was not apparent through the general blackness. Their escape had apparently been carried out most successfully and they were now seated side by side on the horse-block in the Baptist churchyard. The night was warm and cloudless and a little silver crescent of a moon hung just over the high chimney of the old brick church. In the distance, through the spreading branches of a sycamore grove, shone the dim rows of lights of the hotel, and from time to time there reached across the lawn to the young lovers the echo of a waltz from the ballroom, or a low-pitched melody from the negroes at the servants' quarters.

For some moments there had been silence between them. The young man held one of the girl's hands in both of his and at intervals gently pressed the long delicate fingers.

"I hope," said the girl, "that we always shall be known as 'The Bopps.'"

"It *would* be pleasant," the lover replied, "but you know there are a whole lot of Bopps, and beyond the fact that I am engaged to you, I really don't think that I have ever done anything to deserve the title of '*The* Bopp.'"

"I didn't say anything about '*The* Bopp' or '*The* Bopps,'" the girl replied. "What I said was 'The *Bopps.*'"

Bopps nodded his head and said, "Oh!" It was a very weak imitation of a man who understands the meaning of what is being said.

"What I mean is this," said Miss Burden. "If a

46

man, for instance, walks into a club, and another man says: 'Have dinner with me,' the first man must say: 'Thank you, I am dining with the Bopps.' I don't want him to say he is dining with Ned Bopps, or even Amy Bopps. I want that we and our home shall be known as 'The Bopps.' There must be no predominance; our friends must be the same and our personality must be single—never double. Our friends must love us for the mutual atmosphere we create—whether we are at home or visiting. If you ever hear a man say, 'I am going to the theatre to-night with the Billy Wilsons,' you can be perfectly sure that the Billy Wilsons are all right. If he says, 'I am going with Billy Wilson and his wife, or Billy Wilson and Mrs. Wilson,' he had better stay at home —he will not enjoy himself."

Bopps shook his head. "I don't know them," he mumbled.

"Know whom?"

"The Billy Wilsons."

"Now, really, Ned," she said, "there are times when you are very aggravating. I don't know any Billy Wilsons either; they were just imaginary people."

Bopps raised her hand and kissed the tips of her fingers.

"Forgive me," he said, "but ever since you said 'yes,' I have been in a sort of haze, and all I can see is you, just you—whether you are with me or not. I love you so much—I think all day, and most of the night, too, what I can do to show you how well I understand your sacrifice."

This time it was the girl that gently pressed the fingers of the man, and this covert act was followed by a long but pleasant silence. It was finally broken by the girl. "Come," she said, "we must go back to the hotel."

The man looked up into the innocent, pretty, pink and white face with its wonderful halo of yellow curls, then he glanced at the crescent moon, and, with a sigh, rose and followed Miss Burden down the path to the churchyard gate. It was at the girl's suggestion that he left her just before they reached the back piazza, and he watched her disappear alone in the shadows of the old building. But a moment later she appeared again in the lighted doorway of the hotel, turned suddenly and

smiled at an unseen face in the darkness, and once
more disappeared.

Miss Leonore Craig—or, as she was known to her
intimates and through the columns of the society
journals, "Patsey" Craig—was a young woman of
considerable beauty, splendid physical condition,
and a wholesome love for games in the open rather
than those played in the dark corners of hotel piazzas.
She had long been a friend of Amy Burden's and was
now her guest at the Leesburg Springs. The young
women occupied adjoining rooms, and when Miss
Burden stealthily opened her door on this particular
night, she found the narrow bed occupied by her
friend. Miss Craig had apparently interrupted her
own preparations for the night by lying down on the
bed and staring, wide-eyed, at the cracked, whitewashed ceiling overhead.

"Well?" she asked, still staring at the ceiling.

Miss Burden walked over to the bureau mirror,
and, holding up a candle, took a long deliberate look
at herself in the glass. Then she put down the candle
and tried to undo a brooch at the back of the lace
collar of her shirt-waist.

"Well," she said, "I have had him out in the Baptist churchyard."

"I hope you broke it off?"

"Do girls usually take men to churchyards on moonlight nights to break off engagements? I don't. Patsey, dear, will you never get used to the idea of my marrying Ned?"

"I will," said Miss Craig, "when I see the clergyman shake hands with you after the ceremony. I am not looking to you to marry into the nobility—even the American variety; but you are pretty, your position is fairly secure—that is, on the West Side—and you have some money. As long as your engagement is not announced, I shall certainly not give up hope. I am your friend."

Miss Burden took off one of her patent-leather slippers and threw it with considerable force into a neat row of carefully treed shoes at the end of the little room.

"If you were really a friend, you would, instead of finding fault, spend your time trying to get used to him."

"I'll leave that to you after your marriage," Miss

Craig laughed. "In the meantime, I am against Bopps, strong."

"Why?"

"Why?—for twenty reasons. Principally, he is wholly lacking in a sense of humor, and that, I claim, in the case of husbands, is the essential sense."

"I can cure that," suggested Miss Burden somewhat peevishly.

"No, you can't. You can cure a man of drink, perhaps, or the opium habit, or undisguised admiration for other women, but you can't cure him of a lack of humor."

"Perhaps I have enough for both?" There was a touch of irony in Miss Burden's voice.

Miss Craig, still lying on the bed, with her fingers interlaced under her head, smiled broadly. "Any girl who marries a man named Bopps has no humor to throw around foolishly." The speaker suddenly shifted her position, so that she could look directly at her friend.

"Who is the man, anyhow? As a matter of fact, he is the only man at the Springs. I admit, it is something to carry off the one beau here, but for Heaven's sake, don't tote him any farther than the other girls can see you. He may be the only male at Leesburg Springs, but he's not the only man who lives in New York—at least, he wasn't when I left it."

Miss Burden further disturbed the long row of shoes by bombarding it with her second slipper.

"Suppose—I say, suppose I am in love with the man?"

Miss Craig smiled cheerfully. "You don't love Bopps," she said, "you pity him. It may be unconscious on your part, but that's what it is—pity. You are just as sorry for a man with a name like Bopps as you would be if he had been born without legs or if he had a fearful past and had asked you to reform him. You're sorry, but you're not in love. There always was a bit of the martyr about you. Do you remember the time you took up settlement work and the week you spent at the hospital? I only hope this affair will turn out as half-baked as your other charities have. You can resign from sanitary lodging-house boards and hospital visiting committees, but you can't resign from Bopps—not when you are Mrs. Bopps."

"Patsey," said Miss Burden, "you know perfectly well why I gave up those charities. The doctor said——"

"I certainly do know why you gave up those charities," interrupted Miss Craig, "and the doctor had nothing to do with it."

The argument promised to be long. So Miss Burden sat down and tilted her chair against the wall at a dangerous angle. Miss Craig sat on the edge of the bed.

"You quit the hospital because Archie Brewster was in some crazy business with queer hours so that he could call on you only in the morning, and that was when you ought to have been at the hospital. The reason you dropped the settlement game was because your committee was called for the first time the day May Wilson was married to Joe Corcoran, and you said that considering the way you and Joe had played around together at Jamestown, it wouldn't do for you not to be at the wedding—committee or no committee. That's really the cause of all your trouble. You try to make yourself believe that you are naturally serious and a born settlement worker, while, as a matter of fact, you are as full of romance as an Adirondack canoe. If you must marry some one, do wait until you get back to town. Bopps is a case of propinquity."

"He lives in New York," suggested Miss Burden.

"In a way he does," corrected Patsey. "He lives in a boarding-house and he works in Paterson. I know all about him; he's an iron peddler."

"A what? You probably mean puddler, and he's not that. He has a very responsible position in an important brass foundry."

"I've no doubt it's very responsible," Miss Craig sneered—"but I understand it's not sufficiently responsible to trust him with a very large sum of money to take home on pay-days."

"We'll have quite enough," replied Miss Burden. "We have discussed it at length."

"Disgusting," said Miss Craig, rising from the bed. "What's the matter with Sam Ogden? Have you forgotten him entirely? I don't believe you and Sam have been separated for forty-eight hours for the last two years. Has he no rights?"

"Well, if he has, it's all he has got and it's all he ever will have. I'm very fond of Sam, but he's just an idler."

"He's a very charming idler, and he is very much in love with you." Miss Craig crossed the room and opened the door into her own bedroom. Then she turned to Miss Burden, who was nonchalantly swinging her stockinged feet.

"Amy, will you make me one promise?"

Miss Burden shook her yellow hair. "Perhaps," she mumbled.

"Don't announce your engagement until you get back to New York. The night you arrive I will have a dinner for you and Bopps and Sam. Please give Sam that chance."

"Sam Ogden," Miss Burden said doggedly, looking directly into the empty space before her, "is just like all the other young men who play at making a living on Wall Street."

"There is just one difference between Sam and the other young men you speak of," said Miss Craig dryly. "Sam is in love with you and the others are not. Sam is sympathetic and amusing and has a sense of humor, and a cheap spirit of romance, which is just what you crave, although you will not admit it. Bopps has all the instincts of a Paterson commuter. He is sympathetic to you now, because he loves you, but he has no sense of humor. If you marry him, you will regret it within three months, and in six months you will be in love with Sam Ogden. I know you for what you are."

"Notwithstanding which fact," answered Miss Burden tartly, "I am going to marry Ned Bopps."

The answer was an explosive bang caused by the slamming of a door.

II

Like all newly wed couples who live in New York and who are not blessed with unlimited means, the Bopps had been confronted with the eternal question —the choice between a high-ceilinged, derelict apartment on Washington Square and a kitchenette flat in Harlem. They compromised on an apartment on a crosstown street, not far from Riverside Drive, with a restaurant on the ground floor. It was the original understanding that this arrangement was but temporary, but more than two years had passed and the Bopps still found themselves in the same apartment. The drawing-room was a fairly bright little place when the sunlight came through the bow-window and its glow fell on the wall paper with the carmine roses and long green stems; but on this particular occasion there was no sunshine—it was raining in torrents; the drops beat against the panes, the windows rattled in their sashes, and the wind whistled and howled its way through the narrow streets as if it was going to carry away the entire West Side and dump it into the North River. Mrs. Amy Bopps, pretty of face and still slight of figure, stood at a window looking disinterestedly through the mist of the storm to the gray outlines of the towering apartment houses across the way. Miss Patsey Craig, who a little more than two years before had acted as her maid of honor, sat in a deep chair at the fireplace and rested her feet on the steel fender.

"You once remarked, Patsey," said Mrs. Bopps, still looking into the storm, "that Ned had all the characteristics of a Paterson commuter."

Miss Craig extended one foot and gave the coal grate a jarring kick with her heavy walking-boot. "Well?" she asked.

"Well, the Paterson part wasn't necessary. I've

studied the commuter and he has exactly the same characteristics, whether he goes to Jersey, or Long Island, or up Westchester way. He always starts the day by opening his watch and putting it on the breakfast table where the salt-cellar ought to be. Then he defies conversation by hiding behind the morning paper."

"One of these days," interrupted Miss Craig, "when the clergyman says, 'If any man can show just cause why they may not be joined together,' somebody is going to get up and tell the truth and acknowledge that the just cause is a morning paper held up by a carafe of water on the breakfast table."

Amy left her place at the window and the desolation of the storm outside and pulled up a low chair at the side of Miss Craig in front of the fireplace. "What, I object to most about commuters," she said, "is that they all believe they are traffic managers. If there is a crush on the 'L' platform, or a delay in the Subway, or a fog on the North River, Bopps sits down and writes a long letter to the superintendent and asks him what he is going to do about it. My husband's sole topic of conversation every night when he gets home is ferry-boats; whether he caught the *Pittsburg* or the *Altoona* is really about the only thing that interests him. Why, the other day he came home positively in a nervous perspiration because the *Altoona* was going to be laid up for repairs. You might have thought he owned all the dry-docks in Hoboken."

Miss Craig turned in her chair to look at a high Dutch clock that stood in the corner. "What time does he get back?"

"At six—to the minute."

"Is that clock right?" asked Miss Craig.

"It is—regulating that clock is one of the best things Ned does. The winding takes place every Thursday night before he goes to bed. To hear Bopps pull on those chains you might think that he was coaling up an Atlantic liner bound for the Orient."

Miss Craig put out her hand and laid it on Amy's arm. "You poor kid," she said. "Neither of us ever thought my prophecies at the Springs would really come true, did we?"

Amy pressed her thin pale lips into a straight line.

"They haven't—not all of them. You said that in six months I would be in love with Sam Ogden."

"Did I? Well, aren't you?"

"I certainly am not." Amy spoke with an air of much personal conviction.

"Well, you're in love with somebody—and it's evidently not Bopps from the way you play the piano. Women who love their husbands never play the piano that way."

"How do I play the piano?"

"Well, the other day when I was lying down in the bedroom and you didn't know I was listening, you played some music that ought to have been sterilized. It would have made a poetess of passion blush scarlet and knock off work for the day. It was indecent!"

"I have not seen Sam Ogden more than half a dozen times since my marriage, and then only to say 'How-do-you-do,' or 'It's raining," or 'It isn't raining.' He doesn't like me any more."

"He does—he told me so himself yesterday." Miss Craig looked up at her friend and found that the words were not without their result. A new color had come into the girl's face and a new light, or rather an old light, into her eyes.

For a few moments there was silence while the two girls looked down at the four shoes resting on the fender.

"I expect to see Sam to-night." It was Patsey who broke the silence. "He's going to a dance at the Wellmans'."

"Well?" asked Amy.

"Well, I'll tell him that he's foolish; that you're just as good a friend as you ever were and that he ought to come to see you to-morrow afternoon."

Amy interlaced her fingers tightly behind her head and looked up at the tinted ceiling. Miss Craig pulled herself out of the depths of the chair, and with her chin resting between the palms of her hands, sat looking at the burning coals in the hearth.

"All right," said Amy at last. "Tell him I'll be home to-morrow at five." And that was the last time Ogden's name was mentioned that afternoon.

It was unfortunate that on that particular Tuesday Bopps should have returned home with a really unusual bit of local news. He announced that the follow-

ing Thursday evening he had to start on a short
business trip to Pittsburg. It was an event of some
moment, as it was the first occasion on which the
firm had entrusted him with a mission of any import,
and, incidentally, the first time he had left his wife
over night since their wedding day. Of the latter fact
it was Amy who reminded him. On his way up-town
Bopps had secured several time-tables and the after-
dinner hours were devoted to arranging details of
the coming trip. It was finally decided that he should
take a through train, for which the last boat left
Twenty-third Street ferry at five-fifty-five Thursday
afternoon. Amy was to accompany him as far as
Jersey City and then return to a modest home dinner
or dine with Patsey Craig, while Bopps should take
advantage of the dining-car *en route*. In all of this
Amy pretended to take a pretty interest, but down
in her heart she cared not at all. Her mind, even
while she talked of trains and dining-cars, constantly
reverted to the visit of Ogden the next day. Not for
a moment did she admit to herself that she loved him
or ever had loved him—he simply represented a life
that was gone—and gone for good. He was the most

conspicuous of several young men who had proposed to her, and any one of whom she now believed would have been preferable to Bopps. In the days of her engagement she had hoped that these men would remain faithful to her, and from ardent lovers would crystallize into sincere, devoted friends. But in this she was quite wrong. The young men did not like her husband and stayed away. Bopps was fond of his slippers and his after-dinner briarwood pipe, and refused to go to places where a young married woman would naturally keep in touch with her old friends. From the very first she saw that the fight was a hopeless one, and so she settled down to be as good a housewife as her sense of humor would permit. But it must be said that this sense found shape in words only in the long talks with her one faithful friend, Patsey Craig.

Promptly at five o'clock the next day Ogden appeared, and for nearly an hour Amy and he stumbled through the rough-going of the new conditions, but at last the barriers were swept away and they reached the nigh perfect understanding of the days that were gone. At ten minutes to six Amy glanced at the clock.

"In a few minutes Ned will be back," she said, "and before he returns I want to ask you a favor. I would ask it of no one else, because you are, perhaps, the one man who understands me and my whims. I am going to start Ned off to-morrow afternoon, but I shall be back here about seven o'clock and I wish you would take me some place to dinner; that is, if you have no engagement or one that you can break. For a few hours I want you to be very nice and sweet to me, just as if you cared a great deal about me in a silly sort of way—just as if you cared so much that it was hard to talk of anything else but of how very much you—cared; as if it were very difficult not to put your arms about me and whisper to me all you felt for me; but, of course, you wouldn't put your arms about me because in your foolish way you must believe that I am so fine and good and beautiful that you wouldn't dare to touch the ends of my fingers."

"Of course, Amy," he said, "I understand. Where would you rather dine—Sherry's?"

The girl shook her head. "I'm afraid not—we should be pretty sure to meet some one we know."

"There would be a chance," he said, "but it would be the same at the Plaza or Martin's, and it is so much more conspicuous at one of the smaller places. It looks, then, as if you really were trying to avoid people."

There was silence, while the clock ticked off the few minutes that remained to them.

"I'll tell you what to do," he said. "Come to my place. There is only one other apartment in the house, and that's not occupied. The rest of the house is taken up with shops, and they are all closed at six o'clock. There's not a soul about at night except my servant and myself. What do you say?"

"Your servant?" she asked.

"Yes, but that's all right, Amy; I'll send out for the dinner and he can get everything ready and then go out himself. We can wait on each other."

For some moments the girl stood looking at him, but her eyes showed that he was very far from her thoughts. The clock began to strike the hour.

"All right," she said. "I'll be there, but I think you had better make it eight instead of seven. I'll have to come back here to dress. You'd better go now."

"It's awfully good of you. We'll have a fine time. I can't tell you how I appreciate it."

Amy did not answer him, but walked over to the window and stood looking out until she heard the door close behind him.

The following afternoon Amy and her husband left their home at an unnecessarily early hour, but Bopps was an ardent disciple of the "Better an hour too early than a minute too late" theory, and as a result they reached the ferry in time to take the five-twenty-five boat—just half an hour ahead of their schedule. On the way over Bopps was suddenly seized with an inspiration. "I'll tell you what we'll do," he said enthusiastically; "we'll dine at the station. I hate to think of you going back to the apartment and eating all alone; we've plenty of time."

For a moment the rail of the ferry-boat seemed to bob up and down before Amy's eyes, and the deck to heave under her feet as if she were on an ocean liner in a storm. Then everything became normal again and she was conscious that it was necessary for her to combat, and at once, her husband's horrible proposition. And just when everything had been so well

66

arranged! In former years she had often been a guest at little supper and dinner parties at Ogden's rooms, and she knew that as a host he had no peer among her friends. All day she had been looking forward to the wonderful dinner he would have prepared for her, and now it seemed as if she must ruin it all by eating at a station restaurant—with Bopps.

"I simply won't think of it, Ned," she said. "It would be an outrage. You told me only this morning how much you enjoyed those *table-d'hôte* dinners on the cars, and Katie has a nice little dinner waiting for me at home. And you know how it hurts Katie's feelings when I don't eat everything she cooks." As a matter of fact, Amy had planned on her return to tell Katie that she had suddenly been called away to fill a place at a formal dinner at Miss Craig's

But Bopps was adamant—the nearer they got to Jersey City, the more enthusiastic he became over this farewell dinner. As soon as the boat was docked he rushed Amy through the long station to the restaurant.

"Not time to sit down at a table," he said cheerfully. "We'll just climb up on stools at the instantaneous lunch counter and order something that's ready."

Amy accepted her fate as gracefully as she could and climbed nimbly on a high stool at the long counter, but in all her life she had never wanted so much to give way to bitter tears.

"Just the thing!" exclaimed Bopps, looking over the menu. "And something you are very fond of, Amy—chicken fricassee with home-made dumplings."

Amy cast one fleeting look of reproach at the grinning negro waiter as he dashed off after the chicken. All the strength seemed to have gone out of her back, and for a moment she feared that she was going to double up like a jack-knife. It was Bopps's voice that brought her back to the real situation.

"Those crullers down there, Amy, under the cover —to finish off with, eh?"

Amy glanced down the long counter and saw a pile of crullers a foot high; under other glass covers there were pyramids of pound cakes, stacks of sandwiches in greased paper wrappings, and many quarters of many kinds of pie. She wondered at what point Bopps's desire for restaurant food would fail him.

The smiling waiter returned and placed before them two great plates of chicken fricassee. The chicken appeared to Amy to be all legs and each dumpling as large as a grape fruit. Over it all was a most generous supply of heavy yellow gravy.

"One portion would have been enough for two," said Bopps, helping himself.

"For two," said Amy—"for two armies."

Bopps chuckled at her little joke. "And, George," he called to the waiter, "two glasses of milk—cold."

Amy was picking ostentatiously at a small bone.

"What's the matter, dear?" he said. "Don't you care for the dumplings?"

Amy cut into a great mass of dough. "I don't think I am feeling very hungry," she said.

"Now don't tell me you are going to be ill," Bopps said between bites.

Two tears forced themselves into the girl's eyes. The situation had far exceeded her sense of humor. Bopps looked up just in time to see his wife dab her handkerchief into both eyes.

"Poor little woman," he said—"please try to enjoy your dinner. I'll be out to Pittsburg and back before you know it."

In answer Amy only sniffed and blew her nose rather violently. Throughout the rest of the dinner Bopps watched her with much solicitude, and the last chance only to feign eating was lost to her. He had not only made her devour a great part of the chicken and dumpling but a huge slice of lemon meringue pie, for which on other occasions she had, unfortunately, expressed her partiality.

But at last the most unhappy meal of her life came to an end, and Amy followed her husband to the train gate.

"Now don't be miserable," he said by way of farewell, "and don't worry about my giving up dinner on the train. I enjoyed our little party very much."

When Amy arrived at her apartment she found a large purple box waiting for her. She carried it into her room and opened it when she was quite sure that she was alone. She laid the flowers on her dressing-table—they were the first she had received since the day of her wedding. There had been days when purple boxes had been so plentiful that she had regarded them as her natural due; there had been days when her vanity had even rebelled against writing a note of acknowledgment. These were the thoughts that came to her as she stood in front of her mirror with the bunch of damp violets and orchids pressed against her cheek. Half an hour later, when she was dressed, she explained her departure, as she had planned to do, to her two servants. She would see Patsey Craig the next day and tell her what she had done, and thus secure herself against the only source through which her husband might know where she had really dined.

Ogden received her at the door of his study, and she went alone into his own room to take off her cloak. It was the same room that she had known two years before, when she had gone there as one of several well-chaperoned girls. As a married woman she wondered that the bachelor apartment still held the same fascination of mystery for her. At the mirror she carefully arranged her hair and pinned the bunch of violets at her waist and then walked slowly about the room, looking for new faces among the photographs of Ogden's friends. There were several of groups in which both she and he appeared, and, with one exception, he had been standing, in every instance, at her side. The one exception was the picture of her wedding party. She picked the photograph up and looked at it carefully under an electric light. Then she walked back to the mirror. The face was just the same, but the difference between the stiff, high-necked satin wedding-dress with its absurd veil and the low-cut dinner gown she wore now, made her smile pleasantly at the woman in the mirror. For some moments she stopped to look at her reflection. Her black chiffon gown with its steel spangles made a fine foil for the full white throat and the firm, well-rounded arms, the pink cheeks and the hair piled high on the well-poised head.

"Do hurry up, Amy," Ogden called from the outer room, "the dinner is getting cold." His voice recalled her to her position and the absurdity of any attempt on her part to eat another dinner, but she went in and took her place at the little table. It was almost as it used to be—better, perhaps, for, instead of places for six or eight, the table was now set for only two—

the one man that really counted for the moment—
and herself. Such light as there was came from the
four candles on the table; the cloth was almost hidden by American Beauty and Bride roses lying on a
bed of smilax, scarcely leaving space for the wonderful china and glass on which Ogden so justly prided
himself. Amy glanced about the little room and
smilingly recognized the heavy hangings, the mezzo-
tints, the sporting prints, the broad marquetry desk
and the mahogany sideboard, on which there were
many decanters and two silver chafing dishes with
their wicks burning brightly.

She drew the chair close to the table, and, resting
her elbows on either side of her plate, held her face
between both palms. Across the shaded candles
Ogden looked over the smilax and the roses at the
delicately tinted cheeks, the small, straight nose, the
smiling lips, the golden curling hair, the ivory throat
and arms.

"Well?" she asked.

Ogden smiled. "Well," he said and raised his glass.

The girl nodded and, reaching across the narrow
table, touched her glass to his.

"To you!" he said.

"To you, too," she answered, "and to the days that were." For a few moments there was silence, while Amy looked down at the square piece of toast and the caviare on her plate. Then she put down her fork and smiled whimsically at her host. "I suppose I ought to cry, or to try to eat this, or—to do something, but instead I am going to tell you just what happened. Bopps forced me to eat a horrible dinner with him at the Jersey City station about an hour ago. I don't feel as if I could ever look food in the face again. He forced fricasseed chicken and dumplings and lemon pie down my throat the way a child feeds a pet crocodile. It's no use, Sam, I can't eat anything."

Ogden did not attempt to conceal his disappointment. He and his servant had worked hard over this dinner, and it had promised very well.

"Nothing?" he asked.

Amy shook her head. Her eyes were becoming a little misty and Ogden saw that such humor as there might have been in the situation had disappeared entirely. She picked up one of the long-stemmed beauty roses and pressed it with both hands

74

to her lips, which had suddenly become white and straight.

"It almost seems," she said, "as if he might have let me have this one hour of pleasure."

Ogden got up and started to walk around the table to her side, but he stopped half way and leaned against the desk. The girl interlaced her fingers behind her head and stared up at the ceiling, her face white and expressionless.

"There will be other days, Amy," he said.

"No, Sam, there will not be other days. It's no use trying to deceive one's self." Her voice sounded very tired, and she apparently spoke without any feeling of anger or resentment. "If my love of pleasure were half as great as my fear of respectability, there might be many days in which Ned would have no part. I knew that I was going to regret this foolishness when I came here, and I do already. Young women with morals should be more careful whom they marry."

"I do wish," Ogden said, "you would try to eat and drink something."

Amy shook her head. "I couldn't—the memory of

75

Bopps and his dumplings is too evident. Call for a cab, won't you? I must go back home."

"Please, Amy," he begged, "don't go now."

"I have to, Sam," she said. "I just have to. I know it's hard on you, but I wanted to try an experiment and it has failed, that's all. If it hadn't been dumplings and lemon pie, it would have been Bopps in some other form. Please call for the cab."

"You'll let me drive back with you?"

She shook her head. "I would rather go alone. You've been so good to me, please let me have my way just once more."

When Amy got out of the cab she saw the lights from the living-room of her apartment and she knew that her husband must have come back. She had told her servants that they might go out for the evening, and she was sure that they would not return until very late. It was Bopps who opened the door of the apartment.

"Why, Ned," she said smiling. "This is a surprise. Why did you come back?"

"Well," he answered, helping her off with her cloak, "it was like this: Old Burton got back to the office after I had started. You know he has been away on a long trip. I suppose he didn't approve of the deal and so he wired me at Trenton to return and see him to-morrow. I got off and took the next train back. But I didn't expect you home so soon—Katie told me you had gone to Patsey Craig's to a dinner party."

Amy followed her husband into the living-room. Bopps stretched himself at full length in a Morris chair by the side of the centre table and picked up a book which he had been reading. Amy was standing in front of the fire with her hands clasped behind her. As her husband found the page for which he had been looking, he glanced up as if conscious of the eyes that were turned on him.

"How did you find Patsey—all right?"

"I haven't seen Patsey," Amy said. "I didn't go there."

Bopps put down the opened book on the table. "You didn't go there," he repeated. "Why, where did you go?"

Amy half turned from him and the fingers of her right hand closed about a little vase on the mantleshelf. "I was dining," she said, "with a man I used to know. I dined at his apartment."

"Alone?" he asked.

"Quite."

Bopps sat up and put his pipe on an ash receiver on the table. "Why did you do this, Amy?"

"Why?" She picked up the vase she had been fingering and looked carefully at the hieroglyphics on it as if they would give her the reason. "I thought," she said quite dispassionately, "that a little excitement and pleasure would do me good. Don't worry, though—it didn't. I felt really very ill at ease all the time, and that dinner you forced on me at Jersey City had quite taken away my appetite."

Bopps put the palms of his hands together carefully, so that the tips of his fingers touched each other.

"Can't you find pleasure in your own home?"

"Not very much." She crossed over to a chair opposite her husband and sat with her elbows resting on her knees and her cheeks between her palms.

"Who was the blackguard?" he asked. "I want to see him."

"He isn't a blackguard; he's a very nice sort of boy. I invited myself to dinner, so you see it is quite unnecessary for you to see him. That is, unless you want to thank him."

"I don't understand you at all, Amy," he said.

The girl smiled. "I'm afraid you don't. You never did. It is not easy to explain to you, because if you haven't understood in two years, it is difficult to make you understand in a few words now." Her voice was without inflection, and she was speaking apparently to the lamp-globe on the centre table.

"When I married you there were women who told me that the way to hold a man was to keep him guessing, but what's the use if every time you ask him a riddle the man shakes his head and says: 'I give it up.' One trouble about you, Ned, is, that you have no curiosity. Did you ever, for instance, notice this dress I have on?"

Bopps glanced at the black chiffon waist with the steel spangles and hesitated a moment before he spoke. "I—I don't know."

"Well, it's a handsome dress," Amy went on. "I

79

bought it several months ago. It cost a lot of money and I thought it might please you. I wore it at dinner when we were alone here one night and you didn't notice it at all. It didn't even shock you. Really, Ned, it ought to have done that, but so far as you were concerned, it might have been a cotton shirt-waist."

"I work hard all day," Bopps protested, "and often I am tired at night and I can't understand how you expect me to notice everything. You know, after all, that I spend nearly all of my time working for you."

"That's just it, Ned; that's just it. I don't want you to spend all of your time working for me—I want you to squander some of it on me—just waste it on me foolishly. That's why I went out to dinner to-night. I wanted to hear some one say 'I love you.' I wanted to hear a man say that I looked well, that my dress was pretty. I wanted to see a man figuratively on his knees begging something of me; I wanted him to treat me as if I was made of a little finer clay than he was; I wanted to hear a man beg for a favor—not demand it. Since you married me

80

have you ever looked at my calendar? No, I don't mean the calendar on the desk over there. I mean my calendar—the calendar every woman carries in her heart, with certain days marked in red on it. Wedding days, birthdays, Easter, Christmas and foolish anniversary days that should mean nothing except to him and to her."

"You know what I did at Christmas," he protested.

"I do, indeed. You gave me something which you could ill afford. You told me so then, and you have told me of it many times since. I should have been happier if you had given me a Christmas tree which you had dressed with your own hands—if you had only given me a stocking with a foolish toy in it."

Bopps got up and paced the floor, his hands clasped behind his back. "I don't know what you mean," he said, "I don't know what you mean." He glanced down at her, but she looked at him wide-eyed and as if he were something quite inanimate, as if he were a part of the furniture. The clock in the corner began to strike the hour, and for a few moments there was silence.

Amy got up and slowly crossed to the door which led to her own room. "It's Thursday night, Ned," she said; "don't forget to wind the clock." She closed the door softly behind her and crossing the bedroom to her mirror stood listening, with her hands resting on the dressing-table. And then from the living-room came the sound of Bopps winding up the chains of the Dutch clock. Smilingly Amy looked at the face in the mirror before her. "What a kid you are," she said to the blue eyes looking into hers. "What an idiot to talk to a man without a sense of humor."

With her knuckles still resting hard on the dressing-table she pressed her face close to the mirror and looked searchingly into the reflection of her own drawn white features, and for the moment she seemed to be looking into the eyes of all the girls that she had ever known.

"What fools the most of us girls are," she whispered—"what dull, stupid fools! We think we are marrying men, but we're not. They're not real husbands—only janitors."

And then the face in the mirror suddenly became blurred. The girl's arms relaxed and she groped her

THE ESSENTIAL SENSE

way across the room, and throwing herself on the bed, pressed her wet burning eyes against the soft, cool linen. And from the outer room there came to her the sound of Bopps winding the clock.

"THE BAND"

"THE BAND"

I THINK the reason that Philip Barstow and I get on so well together is because we both crossed the prestidigitator's bridge at about the same time. Every one has seen a prestidigitator's bridge—it is the plank covered with red baize that the magician uses to cross from the stage to the auditorium when he comes down among the audience to force cards on us or take rabbits from our inside pockets or coins from our ears. All of us "bachelors" who live long enough must cross the magician's bridge one day and take our places in the audience. The lucky man is the one who makes the transition willingly and in good season. That time usually comes when we begin to meet young women at dinners who look just as their mothers used to look twenty years before— twenty years ago when they married the other man; when we give up tennis for golf and insist that billiards is splendid exercise; when the bumps of our youth develop into rheumatic joints and the safety-valve of our internal machinery is forever sounding a warning to our appetites.

It is not easy for some of us unmarried men to make the transition; there are those—a very few—who, after they have crossed the bridge go back and take up the fight again—even marry. But these are not the true bachelors, the bachelors who were born bachelors, who in their youth carry on most scandalously with every pretty girl in the village, but away down in their hearts know that their finish is a trained nurse and a faithful body-servant.

Barstow and I used to dine together at the club, but we gave that up some time ago. Now we have a little side table at Sherry's or Martin's or even Rector's, where the stage is amply filled and the actors are usually well-dressed and often beautiful, and we can watch their little affairs, and, unknown to them, have our innocent jokes at their expense. In the other days—the days at the club—we talked of ourselves, but that was before we learned that history was not fiction, but fact, and that if ever we did leave this world, the present social structure would go stretching on indefinitely and not come tumbling about the heads of those who were unfortunate enough to be left behind.

There was one thing that worried us a good deal then; and even now, when there is plenty of time between the lighting of our cigars and the hour for starting for the play, we occassionally discuss it mildly. It is a trifling matter of who is going to save our country and effect a compromise with the Trust Senators just before they take our last dollar. Of course, we admit that something is going to save our country—there seems to be a saving factor in our national make-up that always develops when it really becomes necessary. Barstow contends that when the time is ripe the old Puritan blood, the cold intelligence, and the hard common sense of New England will assert itself and straighten things out. But then Barstow was born and brought up somewhere near Boston, and not very far from Concord, and he is just about as narrow as one of his own stone fences. My argument is that the best life—the life that produced the greatest refinement and culture throughout the country, the life that put kindliness and hospitality and brotherly love above money-grubbing—was the life that was pretty thoroughly choked out of the Southern States during the late unpleasantness. We Northerners certainly stamped it out as well as we knew how; but from what I have seen, there is a good deal of it left, and when they learn down there that the war is really over, I believe that the old blood will quicken again, and if it circulates sufficiently far, and in enough different directions, it will do the country a whole lot of good. Of course, Barstow and I have no sectional feeling, and we would like to see every monument that has been raised by either side thrown into the deep sea. It is only the ultimate effect of the blood we worry about.

Very early in July Barstow and I separate; he goes to Magnolia, where he meets nothing but Bostonians, and I go to Virginia, which Northerners avoid because they have a wrong idea that it is hot. When we return in September we swap experiences that are supposed to bolster up our old arguments, and although we have done this for ten years, it has not made any difference in our views. But when I get back this year I am going to tell him my experiences with "The Band" at the Madison Sulphur Springs, which, by way of apology for all that I have said before this, were only made possible by the fact that I had long passed the magician's bridge and was regarded by "The Band" as a mere looker-on.

The Madison Sulphur Springs is not one of those numerous summer resorts in the South which have been rebuilt or restored. It is, in all ways, I imagine, very much as it was long before the war. There is the main building—big and spreading in all its proportions, with a broad porch and high fluted pillars. At one end there is the dining-room, square and severe, with whitewashed walls.

The door at the other end of the piazza leads into the ballroom, which is a little smaller than the dining-room, but equally severe in its lack of decoration. The hotel is surrounded by a wonderful lawn studded by splendid oak trees, and at the left of the lawn there is a semicircle of little whitewashed cottages devoted to the bachelor guests. There are no modern improvements of any kind, but the rooms are immaculately clean and fresh, and the colored servants are the kind who courtesy to you if they are women and if they are men throw their hats on the ground before they address you. Social relaxation is supposed to consist of polite conversation on the piazzas, an occasional game of whist in the hotel parlor, and dancing at night in the ballroom. No simpler life can be found anywhere, and a man who hires a runabout for an afternoon drive over the mountain roads is considered a good deal of a spendthrift. And yet there is something in the wooded hills, the clear blue skies, and the homely life that calls the same people back year after year to this little hotel hidden away in the Virginia mountains. Some of the cabins which once held the overflow of the hotel have been turned into servants' quarters, while others have crumbled into utter disuse; and this would seem to bear out the testimony of the oldest guests that The Springs was once the scene of a greater social activity. Be that as it may, the younger generation of Southern girls still comes there dressed in a simple finery, which, I fear, is often paid for after much saving through the winter months. But the Southern daughter of the old school must still have her month at The Springs, and there the young men still go to pay court to their future brides.

With the exception of two summers, the music at The Springs, during my day at least, had always been furnished by a violin and a piano. However, during one season of great financial prosperity, a cornet was added, and once the orchestra consisted of four young boys, but as they were just learning to play, the music that year was perhaps a little worse than usual. But whatever the number of the instrumentalists, and however great or small their ability, we always called them "The Band," and so, during the past summer, when all the music was supplied by one young woman, we still gave her the same title as her predecessors. The real name of "The Band" was Miss Helen Glenham, a fact which I gathered after considerable questioning from the guests who had preceded me at The Springs. Her contract demanded that she play the piano every morning in the main parlor from ten until eleven, and again in the ballroom at night from eight until eleven. I hope it was not on account of the quality of the music, but it is, nevertheless, a fact that this seemed to be an off season for dancing at The Springs. Occasionally the young people wandered in to the ballroom, and on Saturday nights we organized several rather informal cotillions; but for the most part "The Band" played to an empty room. I must say, however, that she was most conscientious in performing her duty, and during the appointed hours remained faithfully at her post. Whether the ballroom were crowded or empty, one could always hear through the open windows "The Band," with a most fearful regularity, first banging out a waltz and then a two-step, then a waltz and next a two-step.

The first time I saw her, she was resting between numbers, her hands lying idly on the keys. The piano was placed in the corner with the keyboard side next the wall, so that "The Band" sat facing the room, and I could see that she was looking out of a window into the night, and that her thoughts were very far away from the Madison Springs. And then, I suppose, she heard us talking in the doorway, for, without looking up, she mechanically took up a sheet of music which lay at her side, and, putting it on the rack, started to play again. She was a rather delicate-looking girl, fairly tall, with big brown eyes and heavy lashes and narrow arched brows, a fine sensitive mouth, and a nose just a little turned up. This, with a rather high color, gave her almost a suggestion, I should say, of *diablerie*. Had there been a trifle more animation and less of a certain tired look in her eyes, she would certainly, so far as beauty went, have outdistanced any of the alleged belles of The Springs. Her hair was piled high on her head— an arrangement as unbecoming as it well could be— and she wore a simple taffeta dress, which, while well enough made, was modest, indeed, as compared with the clothes of the young women for whom she played.

Later in the evening I was introduced to her, and her manner was, to say the least, but coldly polite. Indeed, I think she rather resented the fact that I had made a point of meeting her. To my somewhat forced and formal remarks she slowly nodded her well-poised head, or spoke in monosyllables, for which I was sorry, because her low, even, Southern voice had a great charm for me. On several other occasions I made an effort to talk to her while she

95

was resting between a waltz and a two-step, but my
success was not more conspicuous than at the time
of our first meeting, and for my pains I was well
laughed at by my fellow guests. They, too, it seems,
had tried to be somewhat sociable with "The Band,"
but had failed as ignominiously as myself. To some
of the women who had asked her to take walks or
to drive with them she had been, perhaps, a little
more gracious than she had been to the men who
met her, but, so far as I knew, she had accepted no
invitations of any kind.

"What she does with herself all day I don't know,"
said Mrs. Simmons one evening as we stood at the
ballroom door. Mrs. Simmons was a whole-souled,
stoutish lady, who wanted to mother the entire
Springs and was usually granted the privilege. "One
never sees her about anywhere. Surely she must
leave her room sometimes except to go to the ballroom, but I certainly can't catch her, and it isn't because I haven't tried."

"It's her way of playing the part," I suggested.

"Well, I don't like her way," Mrs. Simmons
snapped at me. "She's a lady born and bred—at

least she looks it—and, besides, I've heard she was.
But because you happen to be a lady is no excuse for
being a mystery, and piling up your hair on your
head just to make yourself look like a sight, is it?
I'd like to take her in hand. I'd drive one or two of
these young things in their all-lace dresses back to
their Mobile homes. Only last night I asked her to
drive over to Bowl Rock for tea this afternoon, and
she hesitated for at least a minute, as if she were
running over her engagements, and then she smiled
sweeter than anything I ever saw in my life, and
said: 'You're so good to ask me, Mrs. Simmons,
but to-morrow it's just impossible.' I could have
slapped her, and all the time she kept on smiling and
picking out a waltz. You know that droop she has
to her mouth when she smiles? I never felt so fat
and uncomfortable in my life. I don't say she wasn't
nice and pleasant, because she was, but when she
started to bang out that waltz, while I was still
standing there, I was strongly tempted to tell her
that there was no better blood in Virginia than the
Simmonses. But I didn't, because I knew she
wouldn't care, so I waddled out, and I could feel her

eyes going right through my back. I certainly will never ask her to another party of mine. Just look at her now. Why, with that dollar-twenty shirt-waist and that duck skirt, she makes those girls of plumage dancing round there look like scullery maids. I'm crazy about her."

I had been at The Springs perhaps about a fortnight, and had quite given up all hope of knowing "The Band" at all, when quite by accident we became slightly acquainted. It was warm, and I was walking slowly, hat in hand, along a rather unused mountain road, when I saw a white skirt in the shade of a large boulder some little distance from the roadway. I knew that the white skirt must belong to one of the guests from the hotel, and I knew that I must know the wearer, because I knew all of the hotel guests. So I climbed the snake fence, which separated me from the boulder and approached cautiously.

"Good afternoon," I said from the far side of the rock, and before I had discovered the identity of the lady in the white skirt.

"Good afternoon," said somebody whom I knew by the voice to be no other than "The Band." A little discouraged, I walked around the rock and found her sitting with her back against the boulder. In her lap there lay a novel, and her sailor hat had been thrown aside. At the sight of me she smiled, not brightly perhaps, but with the same lovely droop to one side of the mouth that Mrs. Simmons had spoken about.

"Oh, it's you, is it?" she said.

Of course, there are several ways of saying: "Oh, it's you, is it?" but the way "The Band" said it, it sounded to me as though, while she was not thrilled with the sight of me, she was glad it was not one of several others. Somewhat emboldened, I asked her permission if I might sit down. With a nod of her pretty head she granted the request. We both sat tailor-fashion—she against the rock and I facing her.

"Wouldn't you like to smoke?" she asked.

As a matter of fact, I had just finished a rather heavy cigar, and did not feel particularly like smoking again, but her remark was so unusually human and unexpected that I promptly pulled out my cigar case.

"I really feel," I said, "as if I had you at a terrible disadvantage—as if you were quite in my power."

The girl looked up and down the deserted road and beyond to the unending ridges of hills. The mouth drooped into the wavering little smile again. "Yes?" she said.

"You see you have no piano to protect you now, no high pile of waltzes and two-steps to look over, no keys to run little scales on while I am trying to tell you how well you played the last piece of music."

For the first time since I had known her, the girl laughed.

"No one was ever brave enough to tell me that," she said. "Why, my playing has killed dancing at The Springs."

"The piano is not the best in the world," I suggested.

"No, I suppose not, but it is so much better than the one I was taught on!"

"Who taught you?" I asked.

"My mother—that is, she taught me all she knew."

"How long have you played—professionally I mean?"

"THE BAND"

The word brought a smile to the girl's lips. "Professionally," she repeated, "I have been playing three years. But it seems—" then she stopped. "Oh, I don't know how it seems. Why should I talk to you like this?"

"Because I'm old," I replied promptly, "and probably because we get on so famously. You were going to say that those three years seem an eternity."

"Those *three hours* I play in the ballroom seem an eternity, if you insist on knowing just how I feel. You can't imagine how sweet and pretty my little bedroom at the top of the house seems after those three hours. And yet it's a very bare little room."

"You seem very fond of your little room," I suggested; "at least no one ever sees you out of it, except at the piano and in the dining-room. Why aren't you more sociable?"

"Why? Why, because I'm 'The Band.'"

"That's foolish. Isn't it respectable to be a band?" I asked.

"This is a perfectly respectable band," she said smiling. "I'm just as respectable as the clerk of the

101

hotel, and that other very fresh young man who sits at my table and who runs the livery stable. We are all honest workers and are much more respectable than the young men who don't have to sit at our table, but who are supposed to dance instead of paying board. As a matter of fact, I suppose they would earn their bed and board a little more honestly if they could persuade any of the women to dance to my music." She opened the book which she had been reading when I interrupted her, and carefully turned back both covers until they touched her knees. Then she smiled at me and really looked very beautiful.

"I want to tell you," she said, "that I only play for about four months each year. The rest of the time I live in Hodgenville alone with my mother. We are all that is left of the Glenhams, and indeed there isn't much more left of Hodgenville. Hodgenville is a very small place in Virginia, where two trains stop going north every day and two trains stop every day going south. Fortunately for Hodgenville, there is a tank there where the engines take on water. Nothing ever gets off at Hodgenville. Was there anything else

102

you thought of asking me?" She was still smiling cheerfully.

"I thought of asking you to walk back to the hotel," I suggested—"that is, after a while."

"You are a brave man," she said, "to offer to walk down that hill and up the road to the hotel with 'The Band.' You are a brave man even to make the offer, and I admire you for it."

I put on my hat and slowly arose. "Good-by," I said, "you're quite impossible."

"No, you're wrong again"—she put out two long tapering fingers, which for a moment rested in my hardened hand: "I'm not impossible—it's 'The Band' that's impossible."

I shook my head by way of protest, but she did not see me because she was already deeply engrossed in her book. So once more I reluctantly turned away, and with creaking joints climbed the snake fence. I sat on the top rail for a moment to rest, and then I turned to look back at her. She must have foreseen my action, for at the same moment she too glanced up and waved a delicate hand to me. But neither in the manner of the salutation nor in the smile that

played about her lips was there an invitation to
return to her, and so I climbed to the ground and
went on alone to the hotel.

We never met again during the remainder of the
summer; that is, away from the hotel. I am sure she
took good care thereafter to hide behind rocks where
she would be wholly concealed from passers-by.
Several times I spoke to her during the evening when
she was at the piano in the ballroom, but she seemed
to have forgotten our little talk entirely and was, I
think, if anything, more unsociable than before.
And so the summer rolled on and I sat on the porch
with the old ladies and listened to "The Band"
banging out the two-steps and the waltzes with the
same fearful regularity.

It had always been the custom at The Springs to
discontinue the music after the first of September,
and a few of us men had each year arranged some
little benefit for the musicians just before their departure. It was usually a concert, or amateur theatricals, but the style of entertainment really mattered
very little so long as there was an admission fee
charged. It was just a week now to the first of Sep-

tember, and the question naturally arose as to what we could do in the way of a benefit for Miss Glenham.

"You can't do anything," said Mrs. Simmons decidedly. "The girl may be as poor as a church-mouse —and I am quite willing to believe that she is the sole support of her mother—but I'm sorry for the committee which has to offer her the proceeds."

And there the matter rested for that night. The next morning we sat about the porch and talked it over and over again, until I hit on an idea which met with the approval of every one. It seemed to me that, as long as the girl had been playing for other people to dance all summer, it would be a good thing to have one night when she could dance and the rest could play. We decided on the evening just before she was to leave, and started in at once to make the plans. Old Howard Kinney, who had led all the famous cotillions at The Springs for the last twenty years, was, of course, to lead with Miss Glenham; Mrs. Simmons was to arrange the supper, and I was to get the favors. There was a big committee chosen to gather the flowers and do the decorations, and I have never known an event at The Springs which the crowd took up with such real enthusiasm. That night Mrs. Simmons and several other ladies went into the ballroom after the last dance was over and officially asked "The Band" to come to her own dance. Mrs. Simmons told me later that the girl didn't seem to know at first just what they meant, but when she did understand she looked from one woman to the other and then threw her arms out in front of her on the piano and buried her face in them; so they never did hear her answer. As Mrs. Simmons said, they should have known better than to talk to the girl when she was tired out after playing all the evening. But she came down, all smiles, the next morning for breakfast; so the plans for the dance went right along.

It was the first intention to have several of the ladies do the playing, but it was decided afterward to hire the band of four pieces from the Alum Springs from over the mountain. Some of the people from the Alum Springs heard what the ball was all about and followed their band over and gave the dance quite a foreign flavor. The oldest guest admits that there

never was a dance just like that one—and there have
been some pretty famous dances at The Springs, too.
It seemed as if every inch of the old whitewashed
walls had been covered with flowers or green boughs.
There were great masses of asters and phlox and
dahlias hung about everywhere, and over the old
fireplace they had made a sort of canopy of cedar
boughs and fairly smothered it with golden rod.
"The Band" stood under the canopy with several of
the older ladies, and we all filed solemnly in and were
received with great formality, just as if we hadn't
separated on the porch five minutes before. She
looked a little pale at first, but in a few minutes the
high color came back into her cheeks, and the tired
look went out of her eyes, and all that evening they
fairly shone on all of us. She had arranged her hair
differently, too; now she wore it in soft rolls and coils
instead of piling it high on her head, and she wore a
décolleté dress that showed the delicate throat and
well-rounded arms, and how wonderfully her head
was set on her shoulders. It was a nice simple white
gown she wore, with just a dash of black ribbon
about it. I don't know much about women's clothes,

but I thought she appeared quite as well as any one in the room, but at the same time it seemed to me that I had never before seen the other women dress so simply. The music from the rival Springs sounded really pretty well, and the favors which I had had sent on from New York were a great success. There were big hats, which had been trimmed with enormous bows of ribbon and shepherdess's crooks and wands for the girls, and for the men there were little bundles of cigars and imitation decorations, and for the final figure we had favors made of real silver. Of course, Miss Glenham danced all of the time, and her favors were piled many feet high against the wall back of her chair. I never saw any one have a better time, apparently, and after the way she had treated us all during the summer, it was wonderful to see how gracious she could be, and what a wonderful charm and splendid poise she had for a young girl. At last the band played "Dixie" and "Home, Sweet Home," and we all marched out to the porch, where we had a most elaborate hot supper, including a fine claret cup, which Mrs. Simmons herself had brewed. I have never known a party to go off with more go and

zing to it, and it was two o'clock in the morning before we said good-night. "The Band" shook hands
with all of us, men and women, and even now I can
see the tall, lithe figure of the girl as she walked up
the staircase of the hotel, her head slightly bent
above the beautiful rounded throat, a big bunch of
red roses held in the white arms, and half a dozen
men following carrying her favors with them. She
left us the next morning, and I supposed it was to be
the last time that I would, in all probability, ever see
her, because I knew that as "The Band" she had not
been much of a success. But just before she left she
came to me and said that she had a great favor to
ask of me.

"When you go North," she said, "you will have
to pass through Hodgenville about five o'clock in the
morning. I should like to ask you to stay with us,
but for certain reasons I fear that that is impossible.
But the train stops there for about ten minutes to
take on water. If you will let me know the day you
are coming, and think that you could possibly get up
that early, I would meet you at the station. It would
only be for ten minutes, but there is something that

I should like to say to you, and I could say it so much better there."

When at last the time came for me to start back to New York, I wrote Miss Glenham and told her the morning that I should pass through her town. As we did not leave The Springs until about eleven o'clock at night, I lay down on my berth with my clothes on, and told the porter to be sure to wake me at least half an hour before we reached Hodgenville.

The train finally came to a stop, and I think it must have been the last of a long series of jolts that awakened me from a heavy sleep. I turned in my cramped berth, and with drowsy eyes looked out to learn if I could, how far we had gone on our journey. But one window was raised, and that only high enough to admit of the narrow wire screen which one finds in all modern sleeping cars. The window shade was drawn down to the top of the screen, and so my vision was limited to a frame, perhaps six inches high, and two feet in length. There was a little station made of clapboards, which at one time must have been painted red. Over the door there was a kerosene lamp held in a rusty bracket, but the lamp was not lit and, indeed, so far as I could see, there were no signs whatever of life about the place. There was a narrow wagon-road, which ran by the other side of the station, and beyond this a high, uneven grassy bank, and then a field of yellowing corn, which stirred slowly in the morning breeze. Beyond this field there must have been another road, which I could not see, because there, to all appearances, stood the town. The sun had scarcely risen as yet above the horizon, but back of a circle of high pines to the east the sky was a brilliant crimson, which faded to a pink rose color, and then from a pearly gray into the deep blue of the passing night. At the end of what I took to be the village street there stood a little low brick building, and on the ledge of one of the green window frames I could distinguish a lettered tin sign, which showed that it was the office of the town's attorney, or the local medical man. Next to the brick office there was a square building, which might once have been the Manor House of the place. It was purely colonial in its lines, and it was a home that, from its proportions, should have been surrounded by great lawns and spreading trees, but

111

now it was shut in by the other buildings, and the dignity of it was altogether gone. Its every line sagged, the capitals of the porch pillars were missing, the steps had well-nigh rotted away and the walls, which had once been white, were now gray and warped and weather-beaten. Then there came two old brick houses, very high and narrow, with many balconies of highly wrought ironwork. Beyond these prisonlike places there was a collection of low whitewashed buildings, which looked as if they were used for a livery stable. This was apparently the extent of the town. Beyond I could see only untilled fields, broken here and there by clumps of pine trees.

And then I was suddenly shaken roughly by the shoulder, and a very scared and half-awake porter told me we were at Hodgenville. I hurried out of the car and found her standing waiting for me on the bank just beyond the station. She held out both her hands: "It was so good of you to come," she said.

She wore a shirt-waist and a short duck skirt, and her eyes were as bright and her skin as clear and cool as the fresh morning breeze that blew little wisps of hair across her forehead and about her ears.

"THE BAND"

"And so this is Hodgenville?" I asked.

She nodded in the direction of the five houses. "Yes," she said, "that is Hodgenville. The big house that used to be white is our home."

"And there is nothing beyond?"

"Nothing," she said, "but a few big farms. I wanted you to see Hodgenville, so that you could understand just what you did for me—just how much that dance meant to me and always will mean to me."

"I didn't give the dance," I protested. But Miss Glenham insisted that it was I who had suggested it and that I had done most to make it a success, and, looking as she did that morning, it was very difficult to deny her anything.

"I only wish I could take you to the house and show you how we have decorated the hallway and the parlors with the favors, and my dressing-table fairly groans now with all the silver things I got. It made my mother so happy, and I was glad to tell her that it was a Yankee who did it all for me."

I suppose I must have looked a little surprised when she used the word Yankee, because she at once

tried to explain, and I think she found it very difficult.

"You see mother lives so far from the world and
has been out of things for such a long time, and then
you know it is not easy for very old people to forget.
This bank we are standing on used to be the first
terrace on our place.'

I instinctively glanced up at the wreck of the old
house. The girl nodded.

"They used to call it Glenham Hall. It was quite a
showplace then—the lawn ran way down there to
where you see the creek. It was a kind of park, and
here where we are standing mother says there used to
be peacocks strutting about and young deer. I think
it must have been lovely in those days, don't you?"
And then for a few moments there was silence. The
sun was peeping over the pine trees now and the sky
and air were fairly aglow with a warm yellow light
There were insects buzzing all about us, and many
little birds were chirping a welcome to the warm sunshine. It was she who was the first to speak.

"Do you—do you have holly in New York?" she
asked—"I mean at Christmas?"

"Oh, yes," I said. "It comes in wreaths with a large red bow on each wreath."

"Ours isn't nearly so grand as that, but mother and I thought we would send you some about Christmas time—that is, if you would care for it. The woods about here are full of it, and there is so little we——"

She did not finish the sentence, for just then the whistle of our engine sounded and the porter came hurrying around the station to warn me that the train was about to start. From the car platform I saw her standing there on the bank waving her hand-kerchief to me. Back of her were the ruins of the old weather-beaten house, and at her feet were the chickens scratching at the ground where the pea-cocks used to strut. But as she stood there that morning, clothed in the golden sunlight of a new day, a smile on her lips, and her head held high, I am sure that she looked just as fine, just as splendid, as the daughter of her own people, standing on her own terrace, should have looked.

TOMMY

TOMMY

EVER since its formation the Cinderella Club had held its annual dinner on Christmas Eve. That this time-honored custom had been established and had been maintained with the full consent of the five wives, who were content to remain at home and decorate their Christmas trees unaided, spoke volumes for the high standing of the five members.

Years before they had been schoolmates and had played together on the ball team against the rival nine of the academy from the neighboring town. When the school-days were over three of them had gone to Princeton and one to Harvard and another to Yale. But the span of four years of separation was quickly over, and although when they returned to their native town each wore a different fraternity pin on his waistcoat, the five old chums were soon bound together again with a tie which required no solemn oath of secrecy or a tinsel emblem.

The days of play and text-books were over, and

each of the five took up the serious work of life—one became a lawyer, another a merchant, another a broker, and the last two started together on the lowest rung of the ladder in a banking-house and in time one sat in the president's chair and financed great enterprises and pushed an electric button when he wished to consult his old friend, who had been appointed receiving-teller after much difficulty, although he had been backed by great influence.

In the case of the five men, the story of the Scriptures had been somewhat reversed, for it was the one who had received the ten talents who had buried his treasure and had done the least to profit by his opportunities.

"Tommy" Carter, as he had always been and was still familiarly called by his associates, belonged to that type of boy who could have easily stood at the head of his class but preferred to devote his time to base-ball and the extermination of all the rabbits and trout in the neighboring territory. Again, when graduation day came at the end of his college career he was content to be the lowest of his class to receive a degree and bore no malice to the young man who delivered the valedictory address, although Tommy, as well as the professors, knew that it was he who should have had that privilege. It was at Class-Day that he received his reward, for the college student regards laziness as no great sin and hates a "grind." And so when Tommy came on the platform that day to close his college life with a few jocular remarks about the president and the professors of his Alma Mater, he received such an ovation as the campus had never known before. It was that kind of an ovation that lasts a very long time, and begins with hand-clapping and ends with the men standing on their chairs and cheering and throwing hats high in the air, and the old ladies who have sons of their own and the young ladies who have brothers and sweethearts alternately waving their handkerchiefs aloft and drying their eyes. There were even gray-haired professors that day who were afterward accused of having joined in a college yell. For four years Tommy Carter had stood for all that was honest and clean in sport and out of it. On the field he was all grit and fight, but when the game was over there seemed to be nothing left but a woman's heart and a hand that was forever being held out to someone. Whatever the stress and however heavy the weather, the sun, at least for Tommy, was always shining. He joked about the bad coffee at breakfast, and in the class-room a problem in trigonometry was not without its element of humor, and at night he turned low the wick of his midnight oil and went about from room to room, staying just long enough to smoke a pipe, tell a few stories, and thoroughly corrupt any idea of serious study.

The Cinderella Club held their Christmas Eve dinner at a rather elaborate shooting-box several miles from the town. The event was so well known that no other member would have visited the club-house that night even had he felt inclined to do so, and so the five men always had the whole place to themselves, and used it entirely as they saw fit. Of course the dinner itself was the chief event. The table was spread in the hall, which formed the body of the house, and the steward always arranged that the feast should be worthy of the occasion. The menu never varied—there was a special lot of oysters from

Massachusetts and a crate of terrapin from Maryland, while the clear soup and the roast pig were of home production. And then to top off with there was a blazing pudding carried in by the chief steward, who proudly held himself responsible for its being. As an accompaniment to all this, there were special vintages of wines carefully sought out by four of the members during the year and subscribed to the feast as personal offerings. The fifth member was Tommy, and to him was allowed the honor of supplying the punch—a most wonderful concoction of his own brew and a fitting climax to a feast worthy of the club and the Yuletide season.

After the dinner was over and the room had become sufficiently dense with gray-blue tobacco smoke and the servants had been dismissed, each member made a little speech in which was combined all the humor he had accumulated during the past year and each ended with a toast, usually of an intimate and sentimental quality. This function over, the members adjourned to the end of the room, where a curtain was withdrawn, disclosing a miniature Christmas tree laden with more or less humorous gifts from each of the members to the four others, and in addition there were real gifts for the wives at home which came in sealed packages and which were carried home unbroken. The tree was the last of the formalities, and this once ended, the old friends sat about the fireplace and told stories or followed Tommy Carter to the piano and joined in the choruses of their college life or listened to him sing the comic songs of the present day. And so for a few hours the men of business forgot their cares and responsibilities and for the moment became boys again. But as the town clock struck midnight the sleighs were ordered (for this was one of those happy towns where they always have a white Christmas) and the five friends said their good-nights and started for their homes. That the members had never failed to bring their reunion to a happy close at twelve o'clock was their proudest boast and was the tradition which had given the club its present name.

The meeting just ended had been voted by all to have been the most entirely successful celebration the club had ever known. The spirit of good-fellowship had seemed just a little more evident than ever

before and merriment ran high from the very first of
the dinner until Tommy had finished his last song
and closed down the piano on the stroke of midnight. Always the chief merrymaker of the meetings,
he had on this occasion far outshone any of his previous efforts. His speech, which was always the last
because it was sure to be the best, was full of the wit
and anecdote and gentle satire which had made him
famous at college and had given him his present
unique position as an after-dinner speaker, and when
he came to his toast, which was to the ladies, he
turned from humor to a certain sweet pathos—a
gentle appreciation of the wives at home who had in
their hearts a blind confidence in the significance of
Christmas Day, and who were even then decorating
the trees and making such preparations that their
sleeping children should awake on the morrow and
learn to look upon it as the one day of all the year.
And after dinner was over it was Tommy who told
the best of the stories and led the choruses and sang
the latest songs in his own inimitable way. One of
the members, the president of the bank in which
Tommy was employed, believed that he, at least,

could account for the great exuberance of his receiving teller. The bank happened to be one of those institutions which pay moderate salaries and give large Christmas presents to their employees. The past year had been one of unusual prosperity, and the directors had decided to give the employees a whole year's salary as a gift instead of the twenty-five or fifty per cent. which had always been the custom. Just before the dinner had been served the president had called Tommy aside and had presented him with an envelope containing three crisp one thousand dollar notes, which, in itself, seemed to the president to supply ample excuse for Carter's excess of high spirits.

On his return home Tommy had told his young wife of the unexpectedly large gift from the bank directors, and then after a brief description of the events of the annual banquet had gone to bed, apparently as happy and content as he had ever been in his life. The next morning after breakfast the Carters exchanged their Christmas gifts, and among the rest Tommy gave his wife one of the three thousand-dollar notes and asked her to deposit it to her own account and to spend it when and how she saw fit. They had no children of their own, but Mrs. Carter always dressed a tree for some of the poorer children in the neighborhood and it was Tommy's part to act as master of ceremonies at the distribution of the candy and toys. This he did as usual, but when once his duty had been performed he complained of not feeling well and protested that the noisy excitement of the children annoyed him. He put on his hat and overcoat, and having kissed his wife told her that he was going out for a long walk in the cool air.

Mrs. Carter could not understand why her husband did not come back to lunch, and after waiting for his return until late in the afternoon she sent for one of his men friends who had been with him the night previous and told him of Tommy's unaccountable disappearance. The clubs and every resort where he was known were searched, but no trace of him could be found. That night there was a meeting of the Cinderella Club at the receiving-teller's home, and Mrs. Carter took the place of her husband. Women who are brought up in ease and comparative luxury and who have had everything done for them all their lives have occasionally a way or rising to a crisis that surprises men who have been trained to take the initiative. That is the kind of wife Mrs. Carter proved herself to be, and she rose to the crisis of her life with all the strength that lies so long dormant in the fibre of a fine woman. It was the wife who arranged the conduct of the search for her husband; it was she who requested that an immediate investigation be made of his affairs at the bank, and it was she who demanded that the police confine their operations to the limits of the town in which he had lived. Under ordinary circumstances, she argued that he would not have left the city without telling her, and if he had met with foul play the act must have occurred in his own town. If, on the other hand, he had voluntarily left his home, then it was not for her to ask to have him brought back. That he was laboring under any delusion or that his mind was in any way affected was not for a moment considered, by either his wife or his friends. He had not led the life of the man who becomes insane and the idea of suicide would be the last to have occurred to him.

Tommy Carter had dissappeared from his home

and apparently from the face of the earth just as completely as if he had died and been buried. The police could find no clue and his friends and family no possible reason for his absence. His books at the bank were in perfect order and his home life was without a flaw. If he had not made a great deal of money in his short business career, it had been largely due to the fact that he found so much happiness and contentment in life without riches. His loss in a social way, at least, was of much import in his own town, for he was a man who was beloved by everyone who knew him, and there were very few, rich or poor, who did not know him. There were many theories advanced and denied, and several times there came reports of his having been seen in different cities in the East, but the rumors were never authenticated and Mrs. Carter always refused to have them investigated. If she had a theory herself it is quite certain she had never told anyone—not even her husband's best friends, who had proved to be her best friends, too, and who had watched over her with the care of a father for his own child. Carter's place at the bank had been temporarily taken by another man and the honorary positions he held in the city life had gradually been filled. But everyone knew that there was one place that was not filled and never would be, and that was Tommy's place in his own home. They called her "the Widow" now, and even although she never spoke of Tommy, they knew that every night and every morning she hoped and longed and prayed that he would come back and with a word explain it all away and begin life over again; not a better life, but just the same old life that he had broken off that Christmas morning.

The weeks and months passed on, and there came another Christmas Eve and the Cinderella Club met once more at the shooting-box, and for the first time, although there were places at the table for five, only four of the members sat down to the dinner. It may have been the stormy weather that had affected the spirits of the members, or it may have been the empty chair at the table, but whatever it was, the dinner lacked the spontaneous gayety and the unrestrained laughter of former years. Had the four members been quite sure that Tommy Carter was dead and decently buried by the side of his forefathers, it would, perhaps, have been different, but it was the thought that he might still be alive that made the sight of the empty glasses hurt. Outside the wind whistled through the deserted piazzas and through the windows they could see the snow driven along in great clouds across the open country. Inside there came from the broad stone fireplace a splendid warmth and a fine orange light which filled the room from the heavy rafters to the polished floor, and the shaded candles on the table threw a warm glow over the heavy damask and the disordered mass of silver and glass of the finished dinner.

The men were sipping their coffee and had lit their cigars when the president of Tommy's bank rose to make his little speech and propose a toast. As if by mutual consent no word had as yet been spoken of the absent member, but now the servants had left the room and it was in the air that the silence on the subject so near to them all would be broken.

"We have done our best," the bank president began, "to carry off this annual dinner with the good-will and the fun which have always added so much to the previous efforts of our little club. And, as we all know down in our hearts, we have failed signally, and we have failed through no fault of our own. No dinner without Tommy Carter could be quite the same as one with him. Were we at all certain that he is no longer among the living I am quite sure that the one toast of the evening would be to his memory. But we are not sure that he is dead. I, at least, wish I were sure of it. I have tried very hard to imagine circumstances which would make the desertion of his wife and his friends possible, even excusable, and I have failed. But my lost love and admiration for the man, and I am sure I speak for all of you, has but been added to my devotion and love for 'the Widow.' There is no act of kindness and sympathy of which the old friends of her husband could be capable which she has not proved to be her rightful inheritance. As we have missed him to-night, so has she suffered every day and every night. And so my toast is to the best of women—'the Widow.'"

The men pushed back their chairs and rising lifted their glasses, and as they did so the door was pushed wide open and Tommy Carter shuffled in.

For a moment he stopped to close the door against

the piercing wind and the flying snow of the storm. Then he walked over to the fireplace and stood there shivering in the light of the burning logs. There seemed to be little left of the Tommy Carter they had known of old. His ragged clothes hung limply on the shrunken figure, and in place of the clean-shaven, smiling face there was a rough, uncouth beard, and his skin was parched and tightly drawn.

The four men resumed their seats and watched the miserable figure at the fireplace gradually thaw out and return to a semblance of the living. With a shambling gait, he approached the table and dropped into the vacant chair. One of the men shoved a bottle of whiskey in front of him and he poured out half a tumbler of the liquor and partly raised it to his parched lips. Some of the old light came into his eyes as he looked into the tumbler and his features broke into the ghastly semblance of a smile. Then he shook his head, and putting the glass on the table, glanced furtively at the faces of the four men about him.

"I guess I won't drink that yet," he whispered.

"Carter," said the bank president, "we were just

about to drink the health of one who in the time of adversity has proved herself a very wonderful woman. I mean your wife."

Carter nodded and pushed the glass of whiskey a little farther from him. For a few moments there was silence, which was finally broken by the president.

"Have you anything to tell us, Carter?"

"I know what you mean," said Tommy; "you mean has the prisoner anything to say before you pass sentence. I understand. I'm the prisoner, and you are the judge and jury. Well, that's why I'm here. I've given myself up and I want to tell my story; but don't make any mistake—it's not a defence."

Carter, with his elbows resting heavily on the table, began to talk in a whisper, but as he continued his voice gained in volume and power, and as the huskiness disappeared there came back the old tones which his friends had known so well.

"A year ago to-night," he began, "I drove home from here in one of your sleighs, and when the owner got out at his place the coachman took me to my cottage around the corner. I don't know why, but for the first time in my life I resented the use of another

134

He glanced furtively at the faces of the four men about him.

man's horse and I resented his fine house. My own little place seemed absurdly small and inadequate, and after my wife had gone to bed I sat alone smoking and hating everything about me. I hated the things actually in the room, and I hated even the vacant spaces because I wanted to fill them with things I couldn't afford to buy. I hated the poor growing plants I had bought for my wife for Christmas and I could have wrung the neck of the canary who kept singing cheerfully although he was in a cage. For five hours I had been making you all happy; for five hours I had been master, and I imagined I knew the thought that had been in every one of your minds that night. You all wondered that in my life I had not taken advantage of the brains that God had given me instead of being left behind by every fool that wanted to pass me. There was never a man who all through his life has had greater success predicted for him than I have had, and there is no one who has failed so absolutely. You know how it was at school, and you know how it was at college, and you know, God help me, how it has been since then. It was I who was to have the success; and yet when

135

the race began it was I who stood by and watched you all pass me one by one and leave me far behind. Away from my own home I had known success—when I lived in the outside world I had been somebody—at least so it seemed to me that night—and I decided that I would go away into a world that knew my worth and where I should get all that I deserved. The love of my wife and my friends had left me, and in its place had come a great longing to play a big part in a big world. Before I went to bed I prayed that God would take away this ambition and that I might wake on the morrow with only the old spirit of happiness and content.

"It was not the first time; the same thought had come to me before; but it never took hold as it did that night. It gripped me like a vise and urged me on to make good the unfilled promise of the past. I chafed under my own failure and I was jealous of your success—yes, the success of you four—the best friends a man ever had. I wanted to be to you in all things—as I had been that Christmas Eve—your master."

Carter pulled himself to his feet and a strange light

burned in his fevered eyes—the same light that had flamed up a year before and driven him out into the world.

"And the next day," he went on, "the hatred of the things about me was still strong, and the thought uppermost in my mind was to get away—away to the broad life that was waiting for me. And so I left my home, as you know, and I went in search of something big and great, and yet something I could not define even in my own mind—perhaps it was power, or it may have been fame or great wealth—I don't know—but it was something which my life lacked and something that a new spirit in me craved."

Carter suddenly broke into a violent fit of coughing, and falling back into his chair laid his head on his arms, which were stretched out on the table in front of him. The four men sat silent and pityingly watched the emaciated frame shake convulsively under the folds of the ragged clothes. The man sitting at his right put the glass of whiskey in front of Carter, but he pushed it away and started in again, very slowly, to finish his story.

"And what did I find? What did I find? I found

the freedom of the escaped convict. Money, I had in plenty, and everything I touched turned into gold. I tried stocks and I went to the races and I gambled, and I bet my money like a drunken sailor, and I always won. That was good, because I needed a great deal of money those days. I was forever travelling—always moving on in the hope that I would find the big life—the high place that was waiting for me. I had never known what it was to have 'easy' money before, but now my pockets were bulging with it, and I spent it as freely as it came, and yet it brought me nothing. I chased on from town to town, and afterward from one country to another—my eyes were blinded by the colors of the rainbow always in front of me and my dogged brain hurried me on in my search for the pot of gold. And then one night the good luck which had been my evil companion through all my travels suddenly left me—left me alone, friendless and miserable. Budapest it was. I had lost heavily all day at the races, and I tried to win it back at night at a gambling club, and I lost and lost. The cards were human things, cruel human things, that reached out and took my money from me and laughed

"And I cursed the men who grinned at me across the table."

at me. The damned things had no mercy and they took it away from me—everything. And then I cursed them and I cursed the men who grinned at me across the green table. They were poor foreign things with short pointed beards and turned-up mustaches and little decorations in the lapels of their coats, and their fingers were covered with jewels, the fingers that took my money from me, and I cursed out the lot of them for thieves and blackguards. They threw me into the street, and I groped my way along until I came to a café where there was a blaze of lights and the men and women were sitting about little tables and laughing aloud and singing with the band. For a time I sat with them, and in the cool night air my brain got clearer, and I saw things as they really were. In place of beauty I found paint and powder and rouge, and the women smiled like monkeys and the poor wizened men showed their gold and their bank-notes as if to prove that they were really men, and the music itself was tainted with the desire for things which are only material. The whole place breathed of passion and excess and unrest, and it seemed as if the world had returned to the state of animals.

TOMMY

"The next day, with the help of the consul, I got light work on a boat that started me in the direction of my own land. The rainbow had gone—and in its place there was nothing left but a great desire for home and rest and the peace and the content which could never again be mine. There is no use in telling you what happened after this—you can see for yourselves. It was bad enough to suffer as I have suffered, but it isn't the body that hurts—it's the mind—I tell you it's the mind."

Carter put his hand to his head and slowly pulled himself out of his chair.

"I don't want any of you to think that I came here for your sympathy, or your aid, but I just wanted you to know. If there was one place in the world where I might find an empty chair waiting for me I knew that it would be here. If I had opened that door tonight and had found this place filled— I thank you for that, anyhow."

"I think you had better have that drink now," one of the men said.

Carter stopped on his way to the door and held up his hand in protest. "Not yet," he said, "not yet.

140

I've got something else to do. I'm going to town."
He slowly shuffled to the door and went out into the
storm. The four men silently rose from the table and
looked out of the windows on the great white landscape. The road marked by the heavy drifts lay deep
in snow, and along it they watched the solitary figure
of Carter fighting against the storm on his way to
the town.

At the stroke of twelve the annual outing of the
club was officially brought to an end and the four
remaining members climbed into their sleigh and
started to plough their way home over the snow-
filled roads. The bank president held the reins, and
no one expressed surprise or curiosity when he turned
into the street at the end of which stood "the Widow's" cottage. It was not necessary to go all the way,
for from afar off they saw that the little house was
aglow with the light of welcome and good cheer, and
they knew that the prodigal had returned. The bank
president suddenly turned the horses and drew the
long whip sharply across their backs. "God bless
her!" he said; "and Tommy too—damn him!"

It does not take good or bad news very long to

reach the farthermost quarters of a small city, and by ten o'clock the next day everyone in town was talking of Tommy Carter's return. And although it was Christmas Day, and no one seemed to have very much in particular to do, there were no visitors at "the Widow's" cottage. There seemed to be a general understanding that the day and Tommy belonged just to her. As a matter of fact, the bank president did drop in during the evening, but it was only for a moment—just long enough to tell Carter his place was waiting for him at the bank. And the next day there was a long line of depositors which all through the morning passed slowly in front of the receiving-teller's window. There were old business men with pockets full of checks and young clerks with little black satchels and poor old ladies and rich young ladies and many little children, all with gold pieces and crisp bank-notes which the real Santa Claus or just some modern Kriss Kringle had given them the day before. As the long line of his old friends approached Carter's desk each rehearsed silently some word of welcome that seemed the most fitting and affectionate, but it so happened that not

142

one of these little speeches was ever made. But as
a compromise each old man or young woman or little
child, just reached through the window and squeezed
Tommy's hand.

THE GIRL WITH THE GREEN TOQUE

THE GIRL WITH THE GREEN
TOQUE

For many years it has been my custom to journey every Saturday afternoon from New York to the neighboring city of Penn, and then back again late Sunday evening. I am on the most familiar terms with the brakemen and the colored porters, and even the conductors on some of the slower trains occasionally give me greetings. Every milepost, every painted board, is an old friend now, and I have watched the leafless slips along the route grow into splendid trees, or wither away and die, as the case might be; but I have regarded them all with the solicitude of the commuter for his early spring rose bush.

It has been my habit on these weekly trips to patronize the parlor car, not so much for its extra comfort or its extra temperature, raised by the negro porter to that of his old Southern home, but because I find that the double, well polished windows of the chair car make much better mirrors than the single glass affairs of the day coaches. I like to lie back in my hot plush chair, and by apparently looking through the window at the landscape see my fellow passengers at work and at play. I like to watch the Philadelphians happy in the return to their old home, and happy too in the thought that they have escaped safely from the clutches of the money-mad New Yorkers. Sometimes one sees little tragedies and comedies too—there are the partings at Jersey City, and the meetings at the other end of the journey. One afternoon, I saw a woman lose a small fortune at bridge just across the aisle from me; and I remember once having seen the three corners of an eternal triangle sitting in a dismal row, and when the husband corner of the triangle looked out of the window, in a laudable attempt to see where Washington crossed the Delaware, the other two corners kissed each other violently, and then as suddenly fell back into their former dismal state.

The prime incident on the return trip of our car is usually a beautiful and well dressed young woman. Exactly why every Sunday evening an unaccompanied, beautiful young woman, and never the same one by any chance, should choose a train which lands her in New York at midnight, I really do not know; but the fact is indisputable. Sometimes she is a demure young woman who invites our confidence, and sometimes she is a trifle forward, and would seem not so much to invite our confidence as our confidences. In either case she is always the keystone of our parlor car on Sunday nights. Every other woman, every drummer, every Princeton student, even I through my mirror window, watch her movements with as much interest as one does the centre pole of a country circus when a tempest is tugging at the guy ropes outside.

On this particular trip she wore a very dark and very tight fitting blue cloth tailor dress. On the cushion at her feet rested two little patent leather ties, and above these were black silk stockings of cobweb transparency. Her hair was evidently of a most vivacious blond type and curly, but this was almost entirely concealed by a Nile green toque and a dotted black veil. She sat directly opposite me, and beneath the veil I could see bowed lips, about which there seemed to lurk a continual smile, the tip of a somewhat retroussé nose with sensitive nostrils, and a delicate but firmly cut chin and jaw that denoted a strength of will not at all in accord with the smiling lips and the piquant nose. Her eyes and forehead were entirely concealed by the veil. In her hands, gloved in glistening white, she held a magazine; but throughout the two-hour trip she did not open its pages or change the severity of her attitude, except occasionally to cross and uncross the transparent stockinged insteps. When we neared Jersey City she refused the proffered aid of the porter, and unattended and with considerable difficulty put on a long mink coat.

Whether a bachelor should or should not assist a lady passenger with her coat is still a disputed question in my own mind. Should the lady be elderly and homely, I invariably and dexterously go to her aid; but in the case of the truly beautiful I find that my gallantry frequently fails me. I also find the same conditions hold in the case of the lady with the heavy valise. My beautiful neighbor on this occasion had a suit case which she herself carried off the train with the greatest difficulty.

THE GREEN TOQUE

As she toted her heavy burden up the long platform at Jersey City, I could restrain the traditions of my bachelor youth no longer, and, approaching her in my most Chesterfieldian manner and at the same moment doffing my hat, asked if I might not assist her with the valise as far as the ferry. The girl, for she was little more than a girl, stopped short, put down the suit case, and then, raising her veil, looked me over slowly.

"Oh, very well," she said. "Why not?"

"Why not indeed?" I replied in my jauntiest manner; and, putting on my hat and picking up the valise, we started up the platform side by side.

"But I suppose you take a down-town ferry?" she said when we were fairly on our way. Perhaps it was the manner of her saying it, or perhaps it was that at that very moment two drummers who had been fellow passengers on our car passed us, and as they did so nudged each other and grinned at me. Whichever it was, my tone at once lost every trace of its familiarity.

"Madam," I said, "nobody goes down-town in New York on Sunday nights except night watchmen and the kind of people who visit Brooklyn relatives."

The severity of my tone and a certain individuality in my remark must have pleased her, for she laughed most cheerily, and said that her visits to New York had been infrequent, and that she really knew but little of the city.

At this my manner changed again, and assuming a lighter tone I referred to the extraordinary weight of the dress suit case I was carrying. "Pardon me," I said, "but are you carrying gold bricks from your native city, or is it a small case of Schuylkill water, which I have always understood was good only as a substitute for ink?"

"Neither." she said. "That valise contains my diamond dress and many other small valuables."

I remembered indistinctly of once having seen an actress who courted fame and riches through a diamond dress; but from the one brief glimpse I had caught of my present companion I was sure that she was not the same woman. "As long as you have confined yourself to one dress for the trip," I suggested, "you were probably wise in selecting the diamond affair. I more than ever appreciate your confidence in permitting me to carry your valise."

The young woman glanced down at my knees, which had begun to wobble perceptibly under the weight of the heavy suit case, and deliberately chuckled. "It is not really a diamond dress," she said between chuckles—"it's a rather plain black evening affair with a few jet beads very inadequately sewed on the corsage. I call it my diamond dress merely as a reproach to my husband."

"From your remark," I suggested, shifting the valise to my left hand, "you must be married, and to a man who is putting something by for a rainy day."

"A rainy day?" said my unknown friend. "He's looking for a second deluge, and I think he is putting by for a pair of swift motor boats or a twin-screw yacht."

"And the other small valuables in the valise?" I asked.

"Oh, just the kind of junk a girl collects at boarding school and on wedding days and Christmases from a got-rich-quick husband. Nothing but chips, really."

We had reached the ferry-boat by now, and, as the night was clear and balmy and a round, white moon hung over our heads, we both moved as if by mutual consent to a bench on the deck. We were absolutely alone, and after making quite sure of this fact the girl raised her veil and turned her big, blue, sympathetic eyes to the high, narrow buildings across the river. Apparently fascinated by the lights of lower Broadway, she slid along the bench until a stray wisp of her golden hair was blown fairly across my eyes.

"To think," she said, clasping her white gloved hands, "that I should ever come to this!"

"Pardon me, madam," I said; "but do you refer to me or to New York city?"

The girl looked up with pouting lips and eyes so close to my own that I could scarce distinguish that they were laughing at me. At the same moment she slipped her right hand under the sleeve of my unnecessarily heavy overcoat.

"My dear boy," she whispered, "first of all, you must know—" There was a shrill whistle from the pier, an answering hoot from our smokestack; the guard raised the bridges, and with a sharp click

154

threw the folding iron gates across the deck. At the
first signal of our departure the girl jumped up from
the bench, fairly fluttered down the deck, and with
her hands on the gates stood peering into the disappearing wharf. I could do no less than follow.

"There is no one there?" she whispered, still looking at the pier.

"No," I said slowly, for her emotional behavior
had tended to render my most commonplace thoughts
a little insecure. "No, no one, I should say; the wharf
seems quite deserted."

"Then," she said, "boy, we are alone, and we
have escaped."

"Yes," I replied, "we are alone, and you have
escaped. Incidentally, what have you escaped from?"

The girl continued to cling in silence to the gates.

"A man?" I suggested.

"Two men, two men and a woman—myself."

"Aren't you afraid of spoiling your nice white
gloves on those rusty gates?" I asked.

She paid no heed to the suggestion; so I left her
still peering into the night, and slowly walking up
the deck I meditatively lit a cigar.

"Never again!" I mumbled, throwing the match over the rail. "I try to oblige a good-looking girl by carrying her valise, and find myself wholly responsible for an idiot child pursued by two men, one of whom is no doubt her irate husband with a gun."

I had often heard that Philadelphia was famous for its private sanatoriums for patients suffering from nervous diseases. That my recently acquired acquaintance had escaped from such a retreat I had good reason to believe. The only question was how to get her back. Certainly no one could turn that beautiful, smiling, cooing little thing over to the police. As a matter of fact, when in her saner moods, and if it had not been for the husband hovering in the background, she would have been pretty good company. Perhaps she had not escaped from a sanatorium; and besides, a bachelor of uncertain age has not always the number of female admirers about him that he is usually credited with.

A moment later she was at my side, her hand resting on my sleeve. The intense look was gone, and now there were only smiles and dimples and white teeth and wonderful flying wisps of golden hair. She clasped her hands about my arm and led me to the rail of the ferry-boat.

"After all," she said, "why not smile with me, or at least at me? We are both young—and see what a beautiful night it is, and we are alone. Look! there is not a soul on deck." The girl withdrew her arm, and leaning her elbows on the rail rested her chin between the palms of her hands.

"Do you forget," I asked, "that there is a boat leaving that wharf every fifteen minutes? That although——"

"Fifteen minutes!" she interrupted. "Isn't fifteen minutes enough to lose oneself in a great city? It took only six days to make a world. With resolution and a little imagination, what could not one do in fifteen minutes? Why, nearly all of the good and bad in the world has been done in less time than that. Why not ask me if I forget that the name of this boat is the *Pittsburgh;* that the pier just over there is where the Hamburg liners land; that the lights beyond come from the houses on the old Stevens place? But why not for only fifteen minutes forget all this? Do you never try to see things as they should be rather than

as they are? It's a most amusing game. Are not these
stars and that moon, for instance, the same stars and
moon that hang over the Riviera? Why in this darkness should that coal pier over there not be the pier
at Monaco, and those lights just beyond the lights
from the Casino and the Hôtel de Paris?" The girl
once more put her arm through mine, and drew herself close to my side.

"This is our yacht," she said, turning her wistful
eyes upward so that the white moonlight fell full on
them and the bowed lips and the oval cheeks and the
wonderful golden hair; "and there are no guests on
board—no one but ourselves, except the Captain
forward there on the bridge and the sailors asleep
below. The boat's called the *Marguerite*."

"The *Marguerite?*" I asked.

"Yes, the *Marguerite*—that is my name. I wanted
to have it called something else; but you would have
it that way. We are steering straight for Monte Carlo
now, and when they put us off on the dinghy, we
shall walk up the hill, very slowly, arm in arm, just
like two bourgeois lovers, and when we get out of
breath we shall stop and listen to the foolish doves in

the cages. And in the shadows of the trees you will put both your arms about me and whisper to me how very much you love me."

"And then?" I asked.

"Then?" she repeated. For a moment I am almost sure the green toque touched the shoulder of my great coat as she looked up at the stars—stars which I saw now might have shone on the Mediterranean as well as the North River.

"Then? Why then I think we'll go to Ciro's and get a little table on the terrace, and we'll drink to our future; that though the night will change to day, and the summer to winter, and from winter to summer again—that we shall never change—that is, to each other; that I shall always be just as beautiful, and that both of us will be just as sure of each other's love. Of course, being a man, you will want to gamble; but I don't think I'll let you gamble to-night. We'll just sit and listen to the chink of the gold and the droning voices of the croupiers coming through the open windows of the Casino, and to the music next door at the Riche; and we can look down at the tiny waves running up the beach and the lights of our own *Marguerite* at anchor out in the harbor."

"This way to Twenty-third Street! All off!" shouted a deck hand.

We passed over the bridge, along the passageway, and then down the steps that led to the street. I glanced at the station clock—it lacked only a few minutes of midnight.

"And now?" I asked.

For a moment the girl stood silent, apparently confused at the jumble of the traffic, at the crowds hurrying past us, and the noisy shouts of the cab drivers and the expressmen. For the first time, I imagine, she was conscious of facing the crisis of her escapade. She glanced up at me and drew a few short breaths through the always smiling lips; but the misty eyes denied them. The crowd from the ferry-house had passed on and left us alone with a few bawling hackmen.

"We had better take a cab," I said, "and talk it over on our way up town."

While she was getting into the hansom I gave the driver the address of a hotel for women only.

"Where did you tell him to go?" she asked, after we had started.

"To the Dolly Madison Hotel. You will be all right there until to-morrow morning."

"That won't do. It's the first place they would look for me; besides, I have been there before."

"I doubt very much," I said, "if you could get into any other hotel."

The only answer was a glance, a feeble smile, and something that sounded very much like a stifled sigh. Then she settled back in the corner of the hansom, and I leaned out over the doors. A solution of the difficulty did not, apparently, seem very imminent to either of us. For a few blocks we jolted along in silence over the rough pavements. When I next turned to look at her, she had taken some visiting cards from a little bag she carried, and was trying to tear the lot of them in half.

"I had forgotten these," she said. "You see, this is the first time I ever ran away."

"Won't you permit me?" I asked.

"Yes, if you don't look."

I took the pack of cards and slowly tore them in

half. Before I did this, however, I did something which was no doubt most reprehensible, but which at the moment at least seemed advisable. It was something I had not done since the days when I played the guitar and was more or less accomplished in parlor tricks. I palmed the bottom card. As the bits of cardboard disappeared over the wheels of the hansom, the spirits of my young and beautiful friend seemed suddenly to revive, and she gave my arm a distinct squeeze through the heavy overcoat, and sat even closer to me than the narrow confines of the cab demanded.

"Now," she said, fairly laughing aloud, "we are really off."

"Yes," I said, "and no. The situation would be somewhat less complicated if you were less of a lady."

"What you really mean," she said, turning and smiling most frankly at me, "is more of one."

"My good young woman," I replied, "do you consider our present situation? Here we are—two absolute strangers, practically stranded in a large city at midnight. I happen to have a home; but so far as I can see, you will have to take this hack for the night."

The girl looked up at my serious face, pouted her lips like a spoiled child, and then leaned back, and from her corner I distinctly heard the most musical laughter. She was really very annoying, and we were getting well on toward the hotel. I was strongly tempted to produce the visiting card, which I had slipped into my pocket, and threaten her with exposure.

"It is like this," she said, pulling herself out of the corner and resting her arms alongside of mine on the doors of the hansom. "You really have no imagination. Why not spend the night in a hansom? Is there anything so particularly soft about your mattress that you must spend every night on it? Some of these holes in your streets might be filled up with advantage; but this cab is all right. You are quite as narrow as the rules of your hotels that won't give a single woman a room to sleep in. You mean well, and, when properly introduced to a lady, I have no doubt you're a very nice person; but really your mind is not resourceful. From your own conversation

I have an inspiration already. You say that they will not let me into any respectable hotel, and that you have a home. It's perfectly simple—I'll go to your home, and you go to a hotel. What kind of a home have you got?"

"It's a perfectly good home," I said. "It's a bachelor apartment over some shops."

"Neighbors?"

"None," I replied—"that is at night," and it was the truth. "The shops are naturally closed on Sunday, and the only other apartment in the place is vacant."

"You have a servant?"

"Yes," I said; "but he is entirely British and has not indulged in any emotion since Victoria died, and won't again till King Edward passes out. Besides, he does not come until morning, and when he knocks you can shout your orders through the door."

"Good!" she said. "How do you feel about hotel life?"

"Oh, it's all right for one night," I replied, fairly cheerful.

I think the same thought must have occurred to

both of us; for we looked at each other and smiled broadly. "No," she said, "I have not come for life— to-morrow morning I shall lose myself in the great city."

"From me?" I asked.

"Of course; you are nothing to me."

"No," I said slowly, "you are quite right—I am nothing to you. It's just any man and any woman with us, isn't it?"

She turned and looked at me with her big eyes wide open. "Any man and any woman," she repeated—"that's how it is with us."

"Good," said I, and lifting the lid of the hansom told the driver to go to my address.

We stumbled up the long flights of stairs and through the ill-lit hallways; but it seemed to make the little sitting-room look only the more cheerful when we had once reached it. The girl seemed to know instinctively that the most comfortable chair was the large leather one in the corner. She dropped into this, and sat with her elbows resting on her knees and her chin between the palms of her hands. For some moments she remained thus, while I lit the fire. Then when the flames were well started she came over to the hearth, and we stood side by side with our backs to the fire warming our hands. Neither of us said anything; but she looked up at me once and smiled confidently and with perfect understanding.

A photograph on my desk had slipped in its frame, and it was this that first seemed to attract her attention. Slowly pulling at her gloves, she went over to the desk and put the photograph back in its proper place. It was the picture of a girl whom I had always thought very pretty; but she did not seem to notice this—it was only the frame that interested her. She sat down before my desk, took off the green toque, laid it aside, and then ran her fingers over the picture-frames, the blotters, the letter-paper, and the many little things scattered over the desk. Without seeming to change anything, she had brought order out of chaos.

She swung about on the swivel-chair and nodded back at her handiwork.

"See," she said smiling, "the woman's touch."

I went over near where she sat, and leaned against the desk. "Why not go back?" I asked bluntly enough.

THE GREEN TOQUE

The girl picked up a pen, dipped it in the ink, and began drawing little figures on the blotter.

"Doesn't he care for the woman's touch?"

She shook her head and lightly tossed the pen on the desk.

"Is it only because he doesn't give you all the money you want?"

Again she shook the mass of yellow curls, and lacing her fingers behind her head stared up at the ceiling. In those few short moments she had become part of the little room—the room where I spent the better part of my days and nights, where every picture, every piece of furniture, every insignificant detail, had become part of my routine life. It was as if she and I had been talking things over there for many years.

"Do you know my town?" she asked.

"Pretty well. Why?"

"Well, socially speaking, you know Market Street is a good deal like the partition in a Jim Crow car down South. If you live south of Market Street you ride with the white folks, but if you live north you must stick to the people on the other side of the partition. My position was altogether wrong geographically—my people always lived on the north side, and I don't think he really ever had any people himself. Personally he came out of the West—I called him Lochinvar when we were engaged." The girl smiled up at the ceiling.

"And since?" I asked.

"Oh, such a lot of things; but that's over now. When we were first married, I tried to make him believe that with all his money he could jump me over Market Street."

"It's a wide street," I suggested.

The girl pulled herself out of the chair and crossed the room to a little mirror over the fireplace. "Society reporters call it an 'impassable social gulch,'" she said, running her fingers through the golden hair.

"Wouldn't you like something to eat or drink?" I suggested. "I have some crackers and champagne."

"I would," she said, "because they are the only things a woman can eat and drink and look well."

When I returned from the refrigerator in the other

168

room, I found her standing on a chair, setting a picture straight.

"I suppose the other man," I said, "came from South Broad Street—he and his folks?"

The girl turned and nodded.

"And he told you all about the people your husband didn't know, and all about the assemblies and dances you never could get asked to."

"Yes," she said, smiling into the mirror. "In fact, he was a regular South Broad Street Othello. For the City of Brotherly Love, there is a good deal of love not altogether brotherly."

I opened the champagne, and we sat at either side of the desk and began our modest supper. She raised her glass, and her blue eyes smiled at me over the yellow liquid. "To you," she said.

"Did Othello marry, too?" I asked.

"Yes, afterward; a charming doll from his own tribe."

"And that didn't help matters?"

"Not at all; we all four became great friends. We were forever together. Somebody told the doll it was the way to play the part."

"Have you any money?" I asked.

The girl nodded. "Plenty. My husband was away when I left; there happened to be a good deal of money in the house—some business deal he had on for to-morrow."

"Where are you going?"

"Abroad, I should think."

This suited my idea exactly. I found a copy of a morning paper, and turned to the list of sailings.

"There is only one boat leaving to-morrow— the *Deutschland* of the Hamburg-American sails at noon for Genoa and Naples."

The girl pursed her lips and looked straight at me; but her thoughts, I could see, were very far away. "It wouldn't do, I'm afraid—they'd be sure to look for me there. Besides, I'm not ready."

"Leave that to me," I replied briskly. "When my servant comes to-morrow morning, give him a list of the things you will need on the way over, and have him send them by messenger to the boat. I will engage your state-room, and you will find the ticket at the purser's office. You should leave here not later than ten o'clock, drive straight to Hoboken, get on

the boat, lock yourself in your state-room, and stay
there till you feel the engines. Then you will be safe."

During the recital of my plans the girl nibbled
slowly at a cracker, and when I had finished she
nodded, smiled, and raised her glass to the beautiful
bowed lips.

"You seem to make escape very easy. Have you
had much experience in giving first aid to the run-
away?"

"You will go, then?" I asked.

"You have made it seem the only course possible."

I rose to go. "I hope you will find everything you
need here," I said, picking up my hat.

"So soon?" she asked. "And I'm never to see you
again? You see, I don't even know your name."

"Oh, that's all right," I said. "You will find it over
there on the letter-paper. Besides, I'm a permanent
quantity. If you should come back years from now,
you would probably find me still here. I dropped out
of action long ago. This is as good a place as any to
see the world go by."

She poured what was left of the champagne into
her glass, sipped it, and handed it to me. That was

the way I left her—no more words, no more hand-shakings—I don't think we even said good-by. But I have seen her often since, leaning against my desk or standing at the hearth—the trim lithe figure in blue, the golden hair, and the bowed red lips always laughing and letting in a little sunshine to liven the daily grind.

I walked around the corner to the nearest hotel and dropped into the most comfortable chair I could find in the deserted lobby. Then I pulled out the visiting-card from my overcoat pocket. "Mrs. George Hill Newman," it read, and in the left-hand corner, "Tuesdays in November"; in the other, "Over-brook." I knew Overbrook as a suburb where many Philadelphians had their summer homes. I walked over to the operator at the switchboard and told him to get me Mr. George Hill Newman at Overbrook, Pennsylvania. Then I went back to my leather chair, lit a cigar, and waited. I suppose Newman must have been in bed, for I waited sometime. Indeed, I had begun to fear that no one would hear the telephone, when the operator called me, and I went into the booth.

"Is this Mr. Newman?" I asked.

"It is," came in a drowsy and very peevish voice. "What's the matter?"

"Nothing much," I said, a little nettled at my reception. "Marguerite is sailing to-morrow morning on the *Deutschland* at noon. I shall engage your passage, and you can find the tickets at the purser's office."

"Who the devil are you?" said the voice, which had apparently lost all its huskiness.

"A friend," replied I, "and a preserver of the hearth and home."

The answer was a very grating laugh.

"Don't ring off," I warned him, determined to deliver my message. "Please remember that I am paying for this, and if you continue to laugh like a hyena I shall have to pay two charges."

"Excuse me," Newman said; "but these bath slippers are very draughty."

"Your bath slippers are of no possible interest to me," I snapped, "but I do want to tell you that if you don't find Marguerite at first, stick to the ship, for she will be in hiding."

"All right," he shouted, apparently in great haste.

"And I don't mind saying editorially," I called as a parting shot: "This is your last chance for Marguerite."

Notwithstanding his extreme haste, I believe that he would have made at least one more remark; but I rang off.

Smilingly I paid the fee, and smilingly took my key from the night clerk. There was not the slightest doubt in my mind that I had acted in a masterful manner. I was convinced that had I arranged for Newman to bring his wife back to Philadelphia, the old trouble could have only broken out afresh. The twelve days on the steamer would clear things up wonderfully, and I could safely trust the blue skies and the gray green hills of Italy to do what North Broad Street never could or would do. And besides, the Lothario from the Quaker Belgravia would have time to fall in love with his own wife. Seldom have I slept with a conscience more at ease or awakened with a keener sense of content at a day's work well done.

I protest that it was curiosity pure and simple that

prompted me the following day to go to the pier from which the *Deutschland* sailed. I had attended to the tickets and sent a basket of fruit and a bunch of roses, both properly inscribed, to my friend of yesterday. My duty had been clearly performed; but about half-past eleven I decided that I was entitled to treat myself to one last glimpse of the girl who, after all, did owe me for something more than a night's lodging. Under ordinary conditions I started in ample time to reach the pier before they had hauled in the gang-plank; but my trip was a succession of mishaps. Twice I was blocked by the traffic of the West Side streets, and then the ferry-boat to Hoboken developed some internal trouble, and we drifted about in a perfectly foolish manner for many valuable minutes. As a result, I reached the wharf just as the boat was being warped about the far end of the pier. Pushing and fighting my way through the crowd of men, women, and children, all waving to their sea-going friends, I finally reached the pier-head just as the *Deutschland* rounded into the main stream.

For some moments my eyes searched the double line of passengers ranged along the boat rail for the girl with the green toque, and then suddenly through the din of the noisy crowd I heard the low, silvery laughter of my friend. At her side a man leaned over the rail and laughed, too, and waved his hat to me. We were near enough for our voices to carry easily; but the happy situation did not seem to call for any particular remark, and so we continued to bow and wave and smile until the boat had reached mid-stream and the two figures had fairly merged in the indistinct mass of their fellow-passengers.

I stood for a long time after that, believing that I could distinguish the handkerchief of the girl still waving in the direction of the pier end. It must have been a long time; for when I turned I found that the crowd had vanished and that I was quite alone. For a few moments more I remained leaning against one of the white posts, and following with my eye the great thin liner ploughing her way through the smooth waters. Ploughing her way to the Mediterranean—to Naples and Rome and to Florence and Venice—to the land of orange sunshine and smiles and love and pretty much all of the other beautiful things that the past has left us. They were starting on their second honeymoon, and I had done it; and I had been there only to wave them good-by and God-speed. Perhaps, after all, thought I, the bachelor has some niche in the world. Even if he does shun the real responsibilities imposed upon every man, there are certain moments in his monotonous, homeless life when he can make amends, even if it is only to darn an occasional rent in the social fabric.

With a last look at the disappearing steamer, I turned, and as I did so I saw the tall figure of a man racing toward me. When he reached my side he was quite out of breath, and leaned against a post, panting, with eyes fairly bulging out of their sockets and the perspiration flowing from his brow.

"Is that the *Deutschland?*" he gasped at last, waving his hat in the general direction of the disappearing steamship.

"It is," I said. "Did you expect to meet it coming or going?" I did not like his face from the first moment I set eyes on it. He paid no heed to my remark, but sat down on the bulkhead and continued to fan himself violently with his hat.

"I don't suppose you happened to see a woman

with a blue dress and a green velvet bonnet—very blond?"

"I believe I did see some one who answers to that description," I replied. "Do you know her?"

"Do I know her?" he repeated, still too warm to show much emotion. "She's my wife."

"Your what?" I gasped.

"My wife."

"She can't be your wife," I said, "because my lady with the green hat is Mrs. George Hill Newman of Overbrook, and her husband——"

"Wait a minute!" said the man, jumping to his feet. "Don't tell me he was on the boat, too!"

I admit that I was becoming a trifle confused. "I think so," I said.

"Oh, you only think so," he sneered. "Well, you can tell him all right, because he has the meanest face in the world, and a brown derby hat and russet shoes."

"My man had a brown derby hat certainly, and russet shoes, perhaps; but I rather liked his face. Who are you, anyhow?"

"It's none of your business," he snorted; "but I

178

happen to be one Johnson Jewett of Philadelphia, and the blond lady with the green bonnet is my wife."

"Pardon me," I said; "but could you tell me why your wife should carry around Mrs. George Hill Newman's visiting-cards with her?"

"I could if I wanted to," said Jewett, gazing sorrowfully after the little black speck far down the bay. "She and Mrs. Newman always carry each other's cards to leave when they are making formal calls and the woman is out. What's that to you?"

"Nothing," I said.

"Do you suppose I could catch that steamer with a tug?"

"You might," I replied; "but it would only create a scandal. Better have them arrested on the other side."

My new friend sat down on the bulkhead again and slowly wagged his head. "I don't want to get her arrested—I want to get her back home."

"All right," said I, the love of advice still strong within me, "why not get busy with the wireless?"

"Good!" he cried, jumping up and clapping his hat on his head. "Where can I find one?"

"Indeed, I don't know," I replied; but as he started up the pier I called after him, "And if you want my advice, don't save words; be a spendthrift for once in your life—tell her all about things at home."

He wheeled about, and for a moment gazed at me curiously, and then he turned toward the bay. "By golly!" he said with apparent enthusiasm, "I will. I'll spend a whole lot. I think she's worth it."

"So do I," said I; but my friend did not hear me, for I only mumbled my words, and besides, he was then trotting down the pier far beyond the reach of my voice.

THE WHITE LIGHT OF
PUBLICITY

THE WHITE LIGHT OF
PUBLICITY

As the elevator slowly descended from the floor of her apartment, Maury said to himself, over and over again, "But women do not commit suicide!" On his way to the front door, through the gilt and marble hall, the young man stopped for a brief moment before a high mirror, and to the white face in the glass he said, "But women do not commit suicide!"

He repeated the same phrase many times on his way down-town in the hansom, and while he was dressing for dinner, and very often during dinner, and again at a foolish play, where he sat between two young girls who hardly knew what the word "suicide" meant. And later, at supper, where he found himself again between the same two girls, although he talked of many things, the machinery of his brain kept on grinding out the same words over and over again. The only thing that he could compare it to was a great printing-press which he had once seen throwing out copies of a morning paper, until the endless monotony and terrible regularity of the click of the machinery made him want to cry out for something to break and stop it.

Maury, in his short day, had known many women, of many kinds, and since he had left college he had seldom been free from some sort of an affair. Sometimes the girl had thrown him over, and sometimes he had tired of the girl and by gradual neglect had cleared the field for new conquests or defeats. But his experience had shown him that "women do not commit suicide." It was this tradition that finally lulled him to sleep that night, and the same thought was in his mind when his servant awoke him the following morning.

"Women do not commit suicide," he assured himself as he hurried into the sitting-room and picked up the morning paper. But there it was, staring at him in great, black type from the left-hand column of the first page:

BEAUTIFUL GIRL ATTEMPTS SUICIDE

Her Love Repulsed by Well-Known Society Man,
Violet Lonsdale, the Actress, Tries to Take
Her Own Life by Drinking Laudanum

Maury sank into a deep chair at the side of his desk and read enough of the story to know that the girl was still alive, that his name was not mentioned and that the man in the case could in no way be held legally responsible. Then he turned over the pages of his newspaper to the railroad advertisements and found that the next train for Pleasant Bay left in an hour. In half that time he was on his way to the Twenty-third Street Ferry, with a trunk packed for a week's stay in the country. For the first time in his life he had refused to tell his servant where he was going, and his only instructions were to hold his letters and to pay no heed whatever to the ring of either the telephone or the door-bell.

The fugitive found a vacant seat in the forward part of the hot, stuffy smoking-car, where the other passengers could see only his broad shoulders and the back of his head. By the time the train had left the main line and had begun to jolt its way along the single-track branch road, Maury had regained a fair part of his normal composure, and, having lighted a cigar, he opened the roll of papers that he had bought at the railway station and slowly began to read the different accounts of the attempted suicide. As he finished the particular article that he sought in each

185

newspaper he stopped for a few moments to look out at the hurrying landscape. It was late in February, and the ground was covered with great stretches of unbroken snow, and the twigs and branches of the trees were sheathed in ice, and shone and sparkled in the morning sunlight like countless strings of wonderful diamonds.

It was six months now since he had travelled over the same road, but then the stretches of snow were green meadows and studded with wild flowers, and the trees were heavy with summer foliage. The occasional farm-houses, with their white clapboard walls and green shutters, surrounded then by blooming gardens and tangled hedges, now looked as cold and bleak as the snow-fields that surrounded them and shut them out from the rest of the world. With a groan and many squeaks from its joints, rusty from too long service, the train swung around the curve that brought it parallel to the ocean and the unending rows of semi-detached villas of the summer watering resorts. There were very few passengers left now, but, with much panting and grunting, the train continued to stop at every little station, deserted save

186

for the station-master, who ran out to make sure that there were no passengers, to wave a greeting to the train-hands and then hurry back to his stuffy office.

It was past noon when Maury, who was now quite alone in the smoking-car, caught the first glimpse of the frozen waters of the little river that empties itself into Pleasant Bay, which, in its turn, flows on to the sea. A few minutes more and the train drew up before the station platform and the young man jumped out to receive a boisterous welcome from the station-master. This over, he turned toward a very old and rickety carriage. It was the only one in sight, and entirely in keeping with the station itself and the general desolation of the surroundings. As he crossed the platform he noticed, for the first time, that the train had carried another passenger for Pleasant Bay. She was a young woman, simply dressed, in a heavy serge suit, with a boa and toque made of gray squirrel. In one hand she carried a muff of the same fur and in the other a suit-case of apparently considerable weight.

Approaching from different points of the platform, Maury and the girl met at the side of the solitary vehicle. The young man bowed and opened the door of the carriage.

"I'm afraid I'm robbing you." The girl spoke in a very low and sweet and unmistakably Southern voice.

"Not at all," Maury said. "Please get in. I'm sure I can find another carriage; besides, I'm only going to the Riverside Inn. It's a very short walk, and——"

"Why, that's where I'm going," the girl interrupted. "Please get in, and we can drive over together."

Maury took the vacant seat at the girl's side and the carriage slowly started on its way to the Inn. For some moments the silence was broken only by the crunching of the wheels over the beaten snow, and then the young man turned to his companion.

"Are you quite warm enough?" he asked, with a certain courtesy in his manner which Maury had for all women. "There is another blanket in front."

The girl looked up at him and smiled pleasantly. For the first time he noticed the big blue eyes—eyes that seemed to carry a peculiar look of trustfulness in them. "Oh, I'm all right, thank you," she said. "You say it's not far to the Inn?"

"No, not more than a mile. You are a stranger here?"

"Yes, it's my first visit," she said; "but, judging by the reception the station-agent gave you, you seem to be anything but a stranger."

"Oh, I've been coming here during the summer for years. My people had a cottage on the river for a long time, and it's quite a second home to me. I knew the place when there were not half a dozen houses between the river and the ocean. You see it's quite a village now. In summer it's really very attractive—sailing and golf and bathing. This winter-resort idea is entirely new. I haven't even seen the Inn since it has been finished."

It seemed to Maury that every minute added a fresh beauty to the girl. The sharp wind had given a high color to the clear complexion and blew little wisps of bronze-gold hair across her face, which she brushed away with her muff.

"We're almost there now," he said, as the carriage turned from the main road into a narrow one that

189

led through a thick pine woods. The girl smiled her pleasure and nodded the flying wisps of hair and the fur toque in his direction.

A moment later they could catch glimpses of the frozen river through the dark pines, and then a sudden bend in the road brought them in sight of the Inn itself. It was a low building—half hotel, half boarding-house, with broad porches inclosed by glass. Inside, several women and one very ill-looking man sat about in wicker rocking-chairs before a great log fire. In one corner there was a safe and a desk on which were a register and a glass case for cigars. Behind the desk the clerk rubbed his hands and gave them a smiling welcome. The girl took the proffered pen, but, before signing, carefully looked over the names on the open page of the register.

"Didn't Mrs. Osgood Price and her children arrive this morning?" she asked.

The clerk shook his head, and the girl's almost habitual smile relaxed into a frown.

"That's very extraordinary," she said; "but surely you got a letter saying that she wanted rooms and that we would all arrive to-day!"

Again the clerk shook his head and smiled sympa-
thetically at the girl's confusion.

"Mrs. Price?" he said. "I'm afraid I don't know
her. Where would she have written from?"

The girl drew her lips into a straight line and nervously beat a tattoo with the pen on the desk. "Philadelphia—probably from the Rittenhouse Apartments—she always spends her winters there. Is
there another train from Philadelphia this afternoon?"

"Oh yes," the clerk said. "It gets here at 6:05—
just in time for supper."

The young woman seemed much relieved and the
frown disappeared.

"That's all right, then. She'll take that, of course."
She pulled off her gloves and, in a firm hand, signed
her name in the register—"Grace Reeves, New York
City."

"It's really terribly annoying, though," she said,
turning to Maury and handing him the pen. "This
being stranded in a strange hotel, in a strange Jersey
town, is no joke for a girl."

"Couldn't you telephone?" Maury asked.

"Of course, that's it. I can telephone"—and the girl looked inquiringly at the clerk.

"I'm afraid not," the clerk said; "but I could send a message to the telegraph office for you."

"All right," she said. "I'm sure she'll come on that afternoon train, but I'd rather be quite certain."

The telegram was written and sent, and then Miss Reeves and Maury went to their rooms and did not see each other again until they met at the luncheon-table. They sat next to each other, and, while the girl still seemed somewhat annoyed over her predicament, she apparently tried to make the best of it and chatted in a most animated way with Maury and the half-dozen other guests who sat at the same large table. After luncheon Maury proposed that they should go for a walk, and, as a result, they spent the greater part of the afternoon tramping over the frozen roads. They walked to the sea, and for a long time sat on the porch of a deserted casino, watching the waves pounding away their strength on the hard beach, and later Maury showed her through the town and pointed out the places which were of much

interest to him because they had been the play-
grounds of his youth.

Late in the afternoon they returned to the hotel,
but, as it would be quite dark at six o'clock, he volun-
teered to take her to the station to meet her friends,
and she gladly accepted his offer. They drove over in
the same carriage that they had used in the morning,
and when the train pulled in he left the girl on the
platform and, hunting up a newsboy, bought copies of
all of the evening papers. One glance at the head-
lines assured him that Violet Lonsdale was still alive,
and so he stuck the roll of papers under his arm
and started to rejoin Miss Reeves.

He found her standing alone, apparently very dejected and altogether miserable.

"They haven't come," she said, "and it's the last
train." There was a break in the low, gentle voice,
and in the darkness Maury thought he detected a
tear.

"Now, that's all right, Miss Reeves," he said, and
resisted a strong temptation to give her a sympathetic pat on the shoulder. She looked so young, and
so pretty, and so very miserable, standing there in

the twilight, deserted by every one except the young man whom she had known for but a few short hours.

"I tell you it's all right," he repeated with a great show of sympathy. "They'll take good care of you at the hotel until your friends come, and—and, besides —I'm here."

The girl looked up and smiled gratefully through misty eyes. "You'd make such a wonderful chaperon," she whispered, and took a small handkerchief from her muff, dabbed both eyes and put it back.

"Now," she said, "that the worst has happened, and there is no help for it, I'm going to make the best of it." She put her little gloved hand under the sleeve of his heavy tweed coat and started down the platform.

"Don't take that awful hack back to the hotel," she added. "Why not walk? It's such a wonderful night!"

It was a wonderful night. The wind had gone down at sunset, and the air was balmy now, heavy with the sme'l of the pine woods and with just enough tang in it to send the blood hurrying through their veins. Here and there a silver star was pushing its way through the purple sky and the ground rolled out before them, a stretch of frosted roads and white, unbroken fields.

"Fine!" said he; "let's walk by all means." And, her arm still in his, they half ran, half walked, over the hard-packed paths. Part-way to the hotel they stopped for breath.

"And you mustn't tell them at the hotel, of course," she said; "but, just between you and me, you are my unofficial chaperon."

"You're terribly good," he said. "It's fine in you to trust me after knowing me for so short a time, but I think we trust people by instinct. You do trust me, don't you?"

For answer the girl nodded the fur toque, and, in the stillness of the night, Maury heard a faint catch in her throat.

It was some time after dinner when he found Miss Reeves alone in one of the little sun-parlors. She was sitting at a table and by the lamplight was reading an evening paper that he had bought on the train.

"Do put on your things," he said, "and let's go

for a walk. I can loan you a heavy coat, and we'll have a look at the ocean. It's too fine to stay in."

The girl seemed delighted at the idea, and, throwing away the paper, hurried to her room. Half an hour later found them back on the porch of the deserted casino down by the sea. It had been a brisk walk from the hotel, and for a long time they sat in silence, looking out on the long rows of white-crested breakers smashing away on the white, flinty beach.

It was the girl who first broke the silence. She was sitting at the edge of the porch, her back against a wooden pillar and her hands clasped about her knees. Maury was smoking at her feet, his legs dangling over the porch's edge.

"Don't you think," she said, "that we city folk— I mean city folk like you and me, who live in a real city where there is so much good, and particularly so much bad—get a great deal more out of the country—a night like this, for instance—than any one else possibly can? New York is such a degraded place—that is, if you believe all you hear."

"It certainly is," Maury said. "And I suppose the most of it is true."

196

"Now, for instance," the girl went on, "I came back to the hotel this evening, after walking all afternoon, and my lungs were full of clean air, and I hadn't one thought beyond the joy of living, and then, after dinner, I picked up an evening paper and —and, really, it was a terrible shock."

Maury nodded. "I know," he said—"I know."

"Just as an example," the girl went on, "did you read that story about an actress—I think her name was Lonsdale, or something like that—trying to kill herself because some brute had deserted her? He was probably to blame for all her trouble, and then, when she is at death's door, he runs away. Think of a girl caring enough for a man to try to kill herself on account of him! As a matter of fact, if his name ever does appear, it will probably turn out that he wasn't fit to tie her shoestrings." Maury for some minutes continued to swing his legs and look out at the black sea with its rim of silver breakers.

"That is, of course," he said at last, "the logical way, I suppose, to look at it. That is the way you, as a woman, look at it, and that is the way the newspaper insists on looking at it. I know Violet Lonsdale,

197

and I think I know the man in the case, too; and, believe me, I cannot quite accept the point of view of the
newspapers. You see, they think in the way which
will please the greatest number of people—I think to
please myself."

"But, after all," the girl argued, "you admit that
the man was a friend of yours. Don't you think that
the papers are probably less prejudiced in their
views than you are?"

Maury nodded his head and twisted the end of his
cigar slowly between his lips. "For the sake of argument," he said, "let's call the man Brown. Now,
Brown's great trouble is that he is just a little different from his class. It would be absurd to say that he
is naïve, but I think he must have been born with an
inherent belief that all men and all women are good
until he has had some sort of proof that they are bad.
If Brown is assured on the best hearsay that Smith is
sixty per cent. good and forty per cent. bad, he will
try to squeeze the figures to seventy and thirty. See
what I mean?"

The girl nodded. "Yes, I see. I've even known
some people like that, but not in New York."

198

"When Brown meets a foreigner at his club," Maury continued, "he doesn't believe that the man is a card-sharper until he knows that he has made altogether too much money playing cards. Brown also doesn't believe that, because a woman is drawing a salary as a show-girl on Broadway, she is necessarily not a perfectly respectable and presentable person; and, believe me, Brown is no more easily fooled by the grafters than, for instance, you or I are. If they impose on his good nature or his bank account he does not choose to regard it as an imposition. He likes to loan money."

"A very unusual person—your friend Brown."

"Yes, he is rather unusual, and that's another trouble. For instance, his methods with women are different. If he meets some one who interests him— and it doesn't matter much just what class of society or the stage she belongs to—Brown gets really interested. He doesn't send his servant around the corner and tell him to buy the lady some orchids or violets, according to the season. Bless you, no—not Brown. He goes down to a bookshop and fools around until he finds some rare, old book that he likes and he thinks the girl ought to like. Of course, she really doesn't like the book, but she knows she ought to like it, and that Brown gives her credit for intelligence, which is something no one ever did before, and that makes her like Brown. It would never occur to Brown to go to a candy store and send a girl a huge box of chocolates. Brown goes to a leather-shop and has something made especially to suit what he thinks the taste of the lady ought to be, or he goes to a silversmith's and he and the jeweller will spend a day on working up a particular design. Now, you know, all that pleases a girl a good deal; and then Brown's belief in human nature is so perfect that he writes his feelings very freely and very frequently— and Brown really writes a pretty good letter."

Miss Reeves smiled. "Your friend Brown has quite a way with the ladies, it seems. His methods sound wonderful to me, but you have told me nothing as yet that would drive Miss Lonsdale—if that's her name —to suicide."

"Brown would never drive any one to suicide, unless it was Violet Lonsdale. Brown had heard all about the lady for a long time. He had seen her

beautiful, hard face on the stage, and he had heard
very hard stories about her off the stage, but he con-
tended that no one so beautiful could possibly be so
hard. Pulchritude counts for a good deal with
Brown."

"Well?" said the girl.

"Well, Brown started out, full of youthful enthusiasm, to find a diamond in a coal-hole. He treated
Violet Londsale as if she had been a duchess and a
lady, and, I suppose, she couldn't stand the shock."

"Had he always treated her as a duchess and a
lady?" Miss Reeves asked.

"He certainly had, up to the very moment of her
attempted suicide. But when a lady asks a man to
come in to have a cup of tea, on a bright, sunshiny
afternoon, and then, out of the perfectly blue sky,
suggests that, if he doesn't marry her, she intends
to destroy herself, I think it is time for him to take
the elevator and the first taxicab in sight and to go
in whichever direction it happens to be heading.
At least, that's what I did."

"Oh, you're Brown, then?" the girl said. "I wondered."

"Yes, I'm Brown."

"Why did you tell me?"

"Well, in the first place, I didn't intend to, and in the second place, I know you won't say anything about it. I had a good look at your eyes this morning when it was light, and you can't make me believe that a girl with eyes like those could tell anything that she was asked not to."

"Now you are talking like Brown. Why did you run away?"

"Cowardice—rank cowardice."

"Could they have arrested you?"

"Why, certainly not; it was fear of the yellow journals. I have a mother and a few sisters who live a long way from here—bless them. Do you suppose I wanted them to read about me mixed up in that sort of a mess?"

"Why did you come here?"

"Oh, I don't know, except that it was quiet and that I should be near people who knew me when I was a kid and before I knew that there was a Violet Lonsdale on earth. It seems to me a perfectly natural thing for a man to do. If my mother had been nearer,

I suppose I should have gone to her. There are some times when every man wants to get back to his mother or to the place where he knew people when he was a kid."

The girl undid her fingers about her knees and interlaced them behind the fur toque.

"You're a queer boy," she said. "Really, knowing you makes the Lonsdale story more simple. And yet it seems curious that any girl with a record for a stormy life should try to do away with herself on account of a man who had treated her but civilly. She must have had a very emotional nature, even for an actress."

"Yes," Maury said, "it would seem so. But, to be quite fair to the girl, you must remember that my friend Brown is a little emotional himself, especially in the face of so much beauty, because the beauty of Miss Lonsdale is superlative and she is not without a certain feline charm. It is possible, too—and in this I may be doing the lady a great injustice—that Miss Lonsdale may not have stood so securely on the lofty pedestal to which I had raised her."

"You mean?" Miss Reeves interrupted.

"I mean that the distinguished view-point from which it was my pleasure to regard her was not understood, or perhaps appreciated, by the lady. Is it not possible that I was to her like other men, just rungs on the ladder that reached up toward her goal, whatever that goal happens to be? You see that naïve streak in me is pretty evident occasionally. This would not be the first time that an unscrupulous woman——"

"Oh, I wouldn't say that," the girl interrupted. "She isn't as bad as that."

Maury's eyes had been turned toward the sea, but now he looked up with much curiosity at his companion.

"You speak with a good deal of enthusiasm, Miss Reeves," he said. "It isn't possible that you, too, know Miss Lonsdale?"

Miss Reeves, her hands still clasped behind the fur toque, continued to look up at the purple sky. "Yes, I know her." The girl no longer wore the habitual smile, and it seemed to Maury that her face had lost the sweetness and the innocence that he had liked so much. "There's no reason I should deny it now," she said; "I've got what I wanted. Besides, you've been very confidential with me; it's only right that we should both tell our real names, as it were."

Maury took a few pulls at his half-lit cigar and then threw it far away from him skidding across the frozen snow.

"Well," he said, "what *is* your real name, and what was it you *did* want?"

"My name doesn't matter so much. I'm a reporter —I wanted your side of the case."

Maury began to swing his legs again over the edge of the porch, and looked up at the girl as if she were some inanimate thing that he had heard about but never seen before.

"Oh, I see," he said. "Then this friendly, almost personal, talk that we've just had was by way of being an interview?"

The girl nodded, and Maury chuckled aloud.

"My friend Brown certainly is guileless," he said. "Would you call that a good interview?"

The girl dropped her hands to her lap and looked directly at him. "Pretty good—fairly good stuff. The surroundings and all the conditions make it rather interesting." She glanced slowly about her. "You understand—well-known society man, a fugitive, tells his story in a lonely casino at a deserted Jersey summer resort. The main thing is that I found you and that you talked at all. It's what we call a 'beat.'"

"I see," said Maury, and he got up and stamped his feet. "It's pretty cold—no? Don't you think we had better be walking back?" He put out his hand and helped the girl to rise. They left the casino and started up the narrow, deserted road that led to the town.

"Do you want to go to the telegraph station now to send your article?" Maury asked. "Or is it too late?"

"There's no hurry," she said, "as long as no one else has the story. I'm going to town to-morrow morning early. I'd rather have them run it Sunday, anyhow."

For some moments, except for the crunching of the packed snow under their feet, there was silence. It was the girl who spoke first.

"I don't suppose you think much of my sort of work?" she asked.

"Oh, I don't know," Maury said. "Before this I have always looked at yellow journalism as a sort of general proposition. This is the first time that I have ever had a chance to regard it from a purely personal point of view. It's something like murder—the word 'murder' really doesn't mean much until you see the blood of one of your friends, does it?"

Again there was silence between them, and then Maury spoke out with genuine enthusiasm, and as if he had entirely forgotten his own troubles. "You know, Miss Reeves, I believe your profession, properly played, is the greatest thing on earth. Just think of it, the news of the whole world thrown on your door-step every morning, and for one penny—and then the power of an editorial! Why, in one short paragraph an editor can get at more people and do more good than an ordinary man can accomplish in a whole lifetime! Just remember what some of those old-time fellows did—the Greeleys and the Curtises!"

"Then you don't believe in modern journalism— that everything that can't stand the white light of publicity should be shown up?"

"I don't really know much about it," Maury said;

"and what I do know I learned from a great friend of mine, who was a newspaper man, although, perhaps, you who know will say that he was not a typical one. He was a star reporter, and hence was practically mixed up every day with the big, vital thing of the hour, but it seemed to me that he got his relative values mixed. You see, when the rest of the world was asleep he was at work, and *vice versa;* so, that when he wasn't actually at work, there was no one to play with, and he sat about a stuffy office, talking with other newspaper men about Jones's story or Brown's 'scoop'; not the humanity of the real thing itself, and never giving one thought to the ultimate effect of the story on the thousands of people who read it. His whole vision became focussed on the news page of one morning paper, and what the rest of the world did concerned him only so far as it fed that one page. A kind word from the city editor loomed as big to him as a decoration, and his only ambition was to work for his bread and butter and the glory of the man whose name appeared at the head of the editorial page. His one thought was how to defeat the libel law, and he would convict a man, as far as public opinion went, in twenty-four hours that the courts couldn't indict in twelve months. And, in time, he got to believe, just as you have learned to believe, that, without regard to circumstances, any act that cannot stand the white light of publicity should be exposed in the press."

"That is what I believe," the girl said.

"That is what your work has *taught* you to believe," Maury answered. "I hardly think you believed it always."

They could see the lights of the Inn now, and neither of them spoke again until they had reached the porch. Then, as they both stopped, Maury held out his hand.

"Good-night, Miss Reeves," he said. "I'm afraid I won't see you again if you are leaving on the early train.'

The girl slowly c asped her hands behind her back.

"No," she said, and the defiant air of bravado she had worn during the walk home seemed to have left her.

"I couldn't very well shake hands with you. But

you mustn't think I'm sorry—you don't understand, that's all. You consider only the individual—I work for a principle." Then she turned and ran up the steps and left him alone.

Maury sat down on the lower step and lighted a cigar, but almost before he had tossed away the match the door of the hotel was thrown open and he saw the figure of the girl silhouetted against the yellow light from the office. Carrying her suitcase in one hand, she crossed the porch and slowly came down the steps to where he sat, and then, dropping the valise, stood looking out at the frozen river glistening through the black, naked pines.

For a moment Maury hesitated—it seemed almost as if he were talking to a woman walking in her sleep.

"Well," he said, "what is it? Please tell me— please." He got up and moved nearer to her.

The girl tried to answer him, but the words died in her throat. "They've put me out," she whispered at last. "They've put me out of the hotel. I'm only a young girl, and they've thrown me out in the middle of the night. Don't you understand?—they've thrown me out!"

"Thrown you out!" Maury repeated. "Why, what do you mean? Thrown you out—what for?"

"It was that telegram—the one I sent to Philadelphia. They returned it with a notice that the woman I sent it to wasn't known. That made them suspicious here in the hotel, and that blackguard in there says I came with you. He says they can't have people like me in a respectable hotel. Think of that—people like me!"

"Oh, I'll fix that all right," Maury said, and started for the door, but the girl threw out her arm and held him.

"Don't!" she cried. "Don't make it any worse! I can't go back there!"

Maury stood still a few moments and twisted his heel in the frozen snow.

"As a matter of fact, Miss Reeves," he said, "appearances are against you."

"My name is not Reeves!" the girl cried. "My name is Harriet Morton, and my name is all that I've got in the world. Do you know what it means for a young girl to be thrown out of a hotel? It's the sort of thing that sticks to her till her dying day. It's

211

ruin—that's what it means—ruin! I've got a mother who's the finest woman in the world, and all she lives for is her children, and everything that she has left now is pride—just pride in us and the name. When she hears this, it will kill her!"

"Well, that's all right," Maury said. "The people in there don't know your name—they think it's Reeves. I'm the only person that knows, and I won't tell. Come along with me."

He picked up the valise, and the girl, although bent with the ignominy of it all, followed him down the road that led to the village.

"Where are you taking me?" she asked.

"Well—I'll tell you," he said quite cheerfully. "The hotels and boarding-houses are all closed, and I am going to the house of an old native I and my people have known for years. He is the village undertaker and the sexton of the Baptist church, which makes him thoroughly respectable on two counts. I think I'll tell him and his wife that you drove over from Lakewood to join some friends at the hotel; the friends didn't get here and, as you didn't want to stay alone at the hotel, I had brought you to stay

212

with them—you, of course, being an old friend of mine. Good idea—no?"

The girl nodded and they walked on in silence until they were near the home of the young man's friends. "That's it," he said; "there's the refuge—a good place to rest and think it over."

Maury reached the station early the next morning and found Miss Morton busy over a telegram. She smiled at him as he entered, and when she had finished writing came to where he was waiting for her and showed him the message.

"You're sure you want me to read it?"

The girl nodded. "You more than any one else."

This is what Maury read:

DAVID GRIERSON,
  City Editor the Despatch, New York.
  Maury got away late last night. Probably on way to Philadelphia, or may have driven inland toward Trenton. Please accept this as my resignation.   H. MORTON.

"Thank you," said Maury. "I like the last part especially."

The girl took the telegram back to the window and
213

then returned to him. "There are ten minutes before the train starts, Mr. Maury," she said; "won't you come outside?—I want to tell you something."

They walked up the platform and sat down on an empty truck.

"Do you know Billy Hardie?" she began. Maury shook his head.

"Well, he's been one of our star men for years. He has a great friend, named Walter Birch, who used to be with the *Despatch*, but is now press agent at the Casino. Last Sunday, Hardie and Birch had dinner up at Violet Lonsdale's flat. It seems that business at the Casino has been bad and the show had to go on the road. They wanted to cut down expenses and were going to put Lonsdale in the soubrette part, but the trouble was, that no one knew her outside of New York. So they talked it over and——"

"And decided to have her commit suicide," Maury interrupted.

Miss Morton nodded. "And she said that you would be the best victim. Hardie was to do the New York end and I was to follow you and get an exclusive interview. That was easy, because we didn't let any one know who the man in the case was supposed to be. We rather thought you'd get away, so I waited outside your rooms for you, in a taxicab, and followed you to the ferry."

"Very simple," said Maury, "when you know the inside story, isn't it? But I thought they arrested people who tried to commit suicide?"

"Oh, that was easy. She had her own doctor and he never said positively that it wasn't a case of taking an overdose by mistake, and then, besides, Hardie is pretty strong with the police."

"Wonderful! But what are you going to do now?"

"I? There's nothing for me to do. The story is no good without my finding you and getting an exclusive interview. It will just fade away, I suppose."

"But *you* can't fade away," Maury protested,

The girl rose and walked a few steps up the platform and then returned.

"Oh, I don't know," she said; "New York is a big place—there ought to be plenty of work. I think the train will be starting soon."

Miss Morton held out her hand. "Will you shake hands with me now, Mr. Maury?"

The young man got up and took her hand in both of his. "Rather," he said. "I'm mighty glad to have known you."

They started for the train together and Maury helped her up to the car platform.

"I'll be back in town in a week," he said—"that is, if this thing blows over. I wish you would call me up any afternoon—my name is in the telephone book. I'd like to help you look for that job—you know, something quiet and not so much in the white light of publicity."

THE DANCING MAN

THE DANCING MAN

HER hands resting on her narrow hips, Eleanor Blythe stood before the bureau and, with levelled brows, looked at the pretty face in the mirror. Her yellow hair was gathered loosely in a great mass over small, delicate features, and her flat boyish figure was draped in a pink kimono of almost diaphanous texture, and apparently little else. Mrs. Blythe, dressed in the almost equally unconventional attire of a black silk underskirt and an all too short dressing sacque, sat in a rocking-chair across the room and stared dully at her daughter. The bulky figure of the older woman filled the chair to overflowing; her hands lay idly in her ample lap, and she rocked slowly but incessantly.

"Are you going out like that?" the mother asked.

The girl glanced down at the clinging silk kimono, at the inch of bare ankles and the tips of gold-embroidered Turkish slippers. Then she looked back again in the mirror at the smiling, pretty face and the blonde curls, and drew the kimono more closely about her.

"I am," she said.

"Where?"

"To the bath. Do I look as if I were going to a tea or for a ride?—or perhaps you thought I was going to play tennis."

Mrs. Blythe sighed.

The daughter ran her long, tapering fingers through the golden curls, and opening a vanity-box that lay on the bureau, dabbed her nose several times with a miniature powder-puff.

"I think, muzzy," she said, slowly drawing back from the mirror, "I look rather pretty this way, don't you—running across the lawn and in and out among the trees? I really think I look quite like a sprite or a fairy—or something."

Mrs. Blythe glanced at the nickel alarm clock over the fireless hearth.

"There are very few folks about just now. The Springs are always dead at four o'clock. I don't suppose many people will see you."

Eleanor turned and fairly laughed aloud. "You

"I really think I look quite like a sprite or a fairy."

THE DANCING MAN

dear old muzzy," she said. "But you never can tell who is peeping out from the cottage windows."

Mrs. Blythe slowly pulled herself from the chair and started to move cumbersomely across the room. "You'll want a bath ticket, too, I suppose?"

"I never heard that the baths were free on Thursdays, did you?"

The older woman knelt down before a trunk, slowly unlocked it, and after groping about the tray, eventually discovered the tickets hidden under a confused mass of stockings and handkerchiefs. She handed her daughter one of the printed cards, and then counting those that remained, carefully put them back in their hiding-place. "Only four more," she said, and with the aid of the trunk slowly pulled herself to her feet again. "And when they're gone, that's the end."

The girl threw back her head and laughed until the tears filled her eyes. "Oh, muzzy," she said, "you are so funny sometimes. Can't we ever bathe again, really?"

The older woman looked dully into the smiling face of her daughter, and then, as if a little dazed,

221

turned, waddled across the room, and stood with her great broad back silhouetted against the window. Through glazed eyes she looked out on the orange sunlight as it filtered through the trees and threw long shadows on the great stretches of rolling lawn. For a moment her eyes rested on the big white hotel with its red roof and spreading porticos and white, fat, fluted pillars glistening in the golden light.

Some robins were hopping about under an apple-tree, but otherwise the lawn was quite deserted and silent, and the only sign of life was at the Casino, where two old men were dozing with their chairs tilted back and their feet resting on the porch railing. The girl crept noiselessly to the old woman's side, and putting her arm about her shoulders pressed her own cold little cheek against the hot, tear-stained face of her mother. "Is it as bad as that?" she asked.

"Yes, Eleanor. It's as bad as that. We seem to have come to the end. Perhaps a week or two more and there will be nothing—just nothing."

She took her mother's hand and led her slowly back to the rocking-chair, and when the older woman was seated the girl slipped to her knees at her mother's feet.

THE DANCING MAN

"I didn't know, mother," she whispered. "I didn't know we were so near the end. Of course I understood that it wasn't far off, but—but you mustn't say that there will be nothing left. There will be you and me."

With closed eyes the mother put out her arms and drew her daughter toward her. "Yes, little girl," she said, "there will be you and me."

And then with a low sob the daughter buried her face on the broad, soft bosom of her mother, just as she used to do when she was really a little girl.

It was on the same day, and almost at exactly the same hour, when Eleanor Blythe learned just how desperate was her financial condition, that the new dancing man first made his appearance at the Madison Springs.

Janet Hone and Arthur Wayne were on their way to the little village at the foot of the hill where the guests go to register their letters or to buy cheesecloth and red paper muslin for occasional fancy-dress balls and private theatricals. The stranger was standing at the edge of the path, looking on at a tennis match, and as they passed he drew back and, raising his black felt hat, bowed to them with a show of old-time courtesy.

"He's very handsome, too," Janet said as they passed out of hearing. "Looks like Thomas Jefferson in extreme youth, what?"

At the same moment Wayne was thinking, too, how typical the young man's clear-cut features were of pictures he had seen of some of the former great orators and statesmen of the South.

For a moment they stopped while Janet gathered her skirts about her, preparatory to picking her way over the narrow stream that crossed their path.

"Do you think Thomas in extreme youth," she asked, "is from the village, or could he be one of those rare specimens—a new beau at the Springs?"

"From the village," Wayne ventured, and he based his supposition on the young man's much-worn and ill-fitting suit of gray clothes, which Janet had apparently overlooked on account of the cameo face and the straightforward but deferential glance from the stranger's dark eyes.

"Oh, do you really think so?" she sighed, slowly

picking her way across the stepping-stones. "That would be a real calamity. I counted ten couples of perfectly beautiful blondes dancing together in the cotillion last night, all trying to look as if they preferred it that way and as if their mothers wouldn't let them dance with men, even if they had been asked."

Wayne took her ungloved hand and helped her across the last puddle.

"It's good to have a man," he suggested, "even an old one, to depend on always at the Springs—no?"

With an almost imperceptible pressure, Janet dropped his hand and smiled at an apple-tree in a neighboring field. Wayne had his winters quite free, but for several summers he had loved Janet Hone with a very moderate passion.

"You're not so awfully old," she said. "You might be much older and still be rated as eligible—at the Springs."

"That helps some," Wayne sighed, "because I never feel old except at a summer resort. I suppose it's because all the girls appear so very young and—and attractive. In town one never seems to have the time or inclination to resent old age or rainy weather. Do you know that only last night I was thinking that when I first met you, ten years ago at Seabright, you were ten and I was thirty—just three times your age. But now you are twenty, and I am forty—just half as old as I am."

She looked up and contracted her eyebrows in a look of mock perplexity.

"Isn't it terrible?" she said. "I suppose if you had kept on with your calculations, you would have found that in a few years more I would be as old as one of those nice grandmothers who gossip on the hotel porch and you would be a boy making horrible noises with a mechanical toy."

They had reached the village store by now, and while Janet went in to make her modest purchases Wayne sat outside and swung his legs from a molasses barrel and talked town gossip w th some barefooted pickaninnies and a few homeless dogs. On their return they again passed the tennis-court, but the young man with the Thomas Jefferson features had disappeared, and neither of them saw him again until late that evening.

THE DANCING MAN

Since his arrival at the Springs, Wayne had occupied a bedroom in one of the outbuildings, formerly called "The Bar," but now generally known under the more refined name of "The Casino." On the lower floor the bar still existed; the second and only other floor was divided into two bedrooms and one larger room which was furnished with a round table and many cane-bottomed chairs. This was called "The Meeting-Room," and was devoted to those of the male guests who cared less for golf and tennis and dancing than they did for the great American game of draw-poker.

On this particular evening, which was early in August, and when the season at the Springs, to quote the words of the local society reporter, was at its "very height," Wayne had gone to his room to dress for supper. When far advanced in his somewhat ornate toilet—indeed, when just about to add the very last touches which would perfect the whole—the wick of his lamp gave a few dying sputters and went out, leaving him in complete darkness. He lighted a match in the hope of finding a friendly candle, but in this he was disappointed. However, he had heard some one moving about in the next room, and without more ado went out into the hallway and knocked at his neighbor's door.

"Come in, please," said a low voice with a very Southern accent, and Wayne opened the door.

The young man whom he had met that afternoon while on his way to the village he found standing in his shirt-sleeves at the mirror, carefully brushing his hair.

"I have the next room," Wayne said, "and my lamp has gone out. I wanted to know if you could loan me a candle for a few moments."

"Of course," the young man said, "but won't you sit down?"

Wayne could not understand at the time why his host should be so embarrassed and his manner so confused, but his hospitality was evidently sincere, and so Wayne accepted a chair and began the conversation by telling him his name.

"I'm very glad to have the honor of your acquaintance," the young man said. "My name is Blackwood—John Blackwood."

"I hope you have come for a long stay, Mr. Blackwood. I find it much pleasanter having a neighbor."

The young man seemed still more confused at Wayne's greeting, and then suddenly turning his eyes on him looked him slowly over, from the part in his hair to the tips of his shining pumps. The survey seemed to cause him some little amusement, for his lips broke into a most charming smile, and he slowly shook his head.

"I don't quite know," he said, "that is, if all the men dress as—as you are dressed now."

For a moment Blackwood hesitated, and even in the dim light Wayne could see the color come into the Southerner's face. "You see, I haven't got a dress suit," he stammered. "We don't wear them at Sackett—that's my home town. It's a very small place in Georgia."

"That's all right," Wayne laughed. "It doesn't make the slightest difference what you wear. I just happened to put these things on because there is to be a dance after supper."

His statement did not seem to assure the young man, for he looked at Wayne rather incredulously, and shook his head.

"I suppose it wouldn't make any difference to you,"

he said; "but you see it's not the same with me. I'm a dancing man. Of course it's not known, but I get half rates at the hotel if I dance every night. It was the only way I could afford to come here at all."

This sudden burst of confidence somewhat embarrassed Wayne, and he was a little nonplussed as to what to say next, for, as a matter of fact, there is probably no place where there is as much absurd stress laid on a young man's wearing apparel as at the Madison Springs. Blackwood took several steps up and down the narrow room and then sat down on the edge of his bed, absolutely dejected.

"I want you to be quite frank with me," he said at last. "Do all the men in the ball-room dress as you do?"

"To be quite honest," Wayne replied, "I think they do."

For a few moments there was silence

"And the worst of it is," Blackwood stammered, "I can't go back home. You don't know just how much this trip means to—to all of us."

"I'm very sorry," Wayne said, somewhat tentatively.

Blackwood looked up at him, and once more his lips broke into the same charming smile, but there was no smile in his eyes.

"Do you mind if I explain?" he asked.

Wayne nodded his head as assuringly and as sympathetica lly as he could.

"My mother used to come to the Springs a long time ago,' Blackwood began, "and she has always wanted me to visit the place where she had once been so very happy. But that was more than thirty years ago, and she said that, as well as she could remember, the men wore pretty much what they chose, and that it was only the girls who thought of pretty things and finery. That must have changed, for I noticed this afternoon how carefully the men dressed, even those who were playing tennis."

"Yes," Wayne said, "I know of no place where a pair of purple silk socks is so great an asset as at the Madison Springs, and a tie to match is a source of genuine porch gossip. But I do not believe that the lack of a dress suit, or even purple socks, is going to damn you entirely or altogether mar your good time. Don't you think if I opened that door and called down-stairs to the bar, a mint-julep would brighten your point of view?"

But the young man refused to be consoled, and only shook his head. The situation indeed seemed desperate and one with which, apparently, Wayne was entirely unable to cope.

For many moments they sat facing each other, the young man on the edge of the bed and Wayne on the wicker-bottom chair leaning against the white-washed wall. And then Wayne had an inspired thought which, if carried through, would seem to relieve the present difficulties at once.

"In the bottom of a trunk," he suggested, "I have another dress suit, and somewhere a store of linen which I am quite sure will fit you finely. Nothing would please me more than to be your tailor and haberdasher during your stay at the Springs. I brought at least twice as many things as I need."

The young man blushed, protested in a number of quite unintelligible words, to which Wayne promptly replied with sound arguments—and the young man was lost. In less than half an hour John Blackwood stood before his mirror as well, if not better, arrayed than any man at the Springs. In any case it was certain that the same clothes never looked so well on the man who had paid for them. The despondency that threatened the all-important visit and the gloom that had filled the little bedroom half an hour before had disappeared entirely. There was a smile on Blackwood's lips now, as well as in the dark eyes. With his broad shoulders thrown back and his head erect, he seemed to have grown at least an inch in height, and there was an air of independence, even a certain manner of indolent indifference, in his way of moving, that had heretofore been wholly lacking. All of this Wayne noted at the Southerner crossed the room to take one last look at himself in the mirror of his dressing-table.

"Will you have that drink now?" he asked.

The younger man turned from the glass and nodded pleasantly.

"Why, yes," said the new John Blackwood, "I think I will."

Almost any man, old or young, who could dance at all would have been welcome at the Springs, for beaux were all too scarce, but the advent of young Blackwood, looking as he did on that particular night, would have been an event anywhere—that is, anywhere where many young girls who had reached the impressionable age were gathered together. Wayne was not the kind of man who was particularly partial to posing in the somewhat tricky rays of reflected glory, but there was certainly a devilish glint in his eye as, just before the cotillion began, he led his protegè around the circle of dancers and introduced him as "my friend—Mr. Blackwood."

There had been an understanding between Janet Hone and Wayne that they were to dance together, so it was arranged that Blackwood should dance with Eleanor Blythe, who in Wayne's estimation was certainly the second most attractive girl at the Springs. The dance happened to be a particularly elaborate affair, given by a family new to riches as well as the Springs, and, as a consequence, the favors were unusually expensive and showy. It would not have been so easy for Wayne to prove this from his own experience as from the last look which he took at John Blackwood just as the band was playing "Home

Sweet Home." His young friend, still most immaculate in the borrowed high collar and the broad shirt bosom and the wonderfully fitting clothes, was decorated with as many ribbons, sashes, orders and medals as an Indian potentate, and the chair which he had occupied during the evening was fairly loaded down with tinsel junk and bore a strong resemblance to the grotto in a fairy pantomime. And the curious— or perhaps the most human—part of it was that no later than the intermission Blackwood was standing entirely on his own feet, and it is a question if even the young man himself remembered who had fairly plunged him into this vortex of success.

When it was all over and the guests had made their adieux, and after Wayne had left Janet Hone at the hotel door, he started in search of Eleanor Blythe and his young protegè. He met them at the steps, just as they were leaving the piazza on the way to the girl's cottage.

"Good-night," Eleanor called to him, but Blackwood ran back to borrow a cigarette. Wayne gave him the cigarette and offered him a light from his cigar, but the young man said that he had a match;

and as he ran back to join the girl Wayne mumbled something to himself to the effect that he was glad that Blackwood had something of his own.

For some moments he stood on the piazza, which was now almost deserted, looking out at the two figures as they disappeared into the darkness. Then he heard a low chuckle, and looking about saw his old friend, Peter Addicks, standing at his side.

"I want to take one turn before I go to bed," he said, and he put his arm through that of Wayne. Addicks was the youngest of all old men, and his knowledge of Madison Springs was much greater and went back further than that of any of its other guests. He lighted a cigar and tossed the match over the railing.

"Who is your young friend?" he asked, as they started to walk up the piazza.

"Blackwood," Wayne said, "John Blackwood."

"Blackwood?" Addicks repeated, "Blackwood? Of course—he must be a son of old Jack Blackwood down in Gordon County, Georgia. How curious— looks like him, too. Do you know if the old man or his mother is alive?"

"The mother is," Wayne said.

Addicks stopped for a moment while he took a stronger grip on the younger man's arm.

"Ah, my boy, there was a woman for you—one in ten thousand. Mary Bent she was then—the toast of the Springs in those days, and we all wanted to marry her, but Jack did the trick, and he had less to marry on than the most of us. This boy looks a good deal like him—same eyes and clean-cut features, and the same manner, too. And, my boy, if you could have seen him play poker! It was a treat to watch that man bluff—the greatest card-player I ever saw."

They stopped in their walk, and leaning on the balustrade, looked out at the twinkling lights from the circle of cottages across the lawn.

"Has the boy money?" he asked.

For a moment Wayne hesitated, but having already clothed his young friend in the finest raiment, he saw no particular reason at the time why he should not adorn him with all the other virtues. "Why—why, yes," he said, "I believe he has—a good deal."

"He certainly dresses as if he had," Addicks mumbled. "Funny, too, because it's hard to imagine a Blackwood with money. Still, you never can tell nowadays, when they make millionaires overnight. I think I'll be off to bed."

"You won't finish your cigar at the Meeting-Room?"

Addicks chuckled. "Not me—I'm too old for cards. Good-night, and keep your eye on young Blackwood. If he can bluff like his father he'll have all the money in the place in no time—and that isn't the worst he'll do, either. Good-night to you."

Wayne went over to his bedroom at the Casino, put on a smoking-jacket, and then crossed the hall to the Meeting-Room, where he found half a dozen men seated at the round table and the game already well under way. He had just succeeded in refusing a general and very urgent request to join the game, and had drawn up a chair behind one of the men, when the door opened and Blackwood came in. He was introduced to the men he had not already met at the dance and took a seat back of the players next to Wayne.

"Won't you join us, Mr. Blackwood?" one of the men said; "seven make a good game."

238

THE DANCING MAN

For a moment Blackwood hesitated and then, unseen by the others, Wayne pressed a roll of bills into his hand, and the newcomer said that nothing would give him greater pleasure than to join so distinguished a party, and he said it, too, as if he meant it.

For half an hour Wayne, with ever-increasing admiration, looked on at the manner in which his protegè played poker. Never before had he seen such an exhibition of reckless daring and cold nerve. In the hands of the Southerner deuces assumed the dignity of aces, and, as manipulated by this arch-expert, a pair of treys seemed to possess the same winning qualities as a king full. The player's face was as mobile as a French comedian's and as unintelligible as that of the Sphinx, and it was with a genuine feeling of reluctance that Wayne finally convinced himself that it was time for bed.

"Go as far as you like," he whispered to Blackwood, and then, after a general "good-night," he left the room with an easy conscience as to the fate of his recently invested capital.

It is possible that, had he known the heights to which the limit of the game was finally raised, he would not have slept with the same tranquillity which he actually enjoyed. For, before the lamps spluttered out and the shutters were opened to let in the gray uncertain light of early morning on the six tired, haggard faces of six men who were trying to "get back," the game had assumed proportions heretofore unknown at the Springs—proportions as detrimental to the nervous system and the tranquillity of a summer resort as to the pocketbooks of those most actively interested. Tales of that night and the amount of money that changed hands are still spoken of in the darkest corners of the hotel piazzas, and always in whispers, and while the exact amount which the debonair and fascinating Mr. Blackwood really did take away that gray morning has never been known, it has nevertheless grown, in each telling, to the most splendid proportions. Whatever the exact amount may have been, there is no question that about seven o'clock in the morning Blackwood, with his face a li tle pale but with bright eyes, and still looking most immaculate in evening attire, appeared at the bedside of Arthur Wayne and gently shook him into a state of partial consciousness.

"There's your money," he said, and laid Wayne's original roll of bills on the table at the bedside. "I didn't need it, as things turned out."

Wayne pulled himself to a sitting posture and blinked at his early visitor.

"That's all right," he said, "but I wasn't in such an awful hurry for the money that I couldn't wait until a respectable hour for it."

Blackwood smiled pleasantly. "I understand that, of course," he replied, speaking with his slow Georgian accent, "but I knew that you would be glad to hear that I was going to explain to the clerk at the hotel as soon as he gets up that I was able to pay regular board. You and he are the only people who know, and I think I can fix him. You see, with this money I won, I've graduated from the dancing-man class."

"Good," Wayne yawned, "but even that interesting news seems hardly sufficient cause for such a very early call. What time is it, anyhow?"

"About seven," Blackwood drawled; "but as a matter of fact, that wasn't what I wanted most to see you about. In the confusion last night I asked Miss

241

Blythe to go riding at eight this morning. You know
—a little ride before breakfast to get up an appetite
—and, unfortunately, I haven't any riding things.
Could you——?"

In silence Wayne threw back the bedclothes, and
going to a curtain hung across a row of hooks which
were fastened to the whitewashed wall, took down
a pair of riding-breeches and then, and still in silence, fumbled about in a deep trunk until he had
found a well-varnished pair of leggings.

"That will do finely," Blackwood said, critically
examining his new possessions. "Now for a plunge
in the cold pool and I shall be feeling all right again.
Much obliged. Very nice girl, that Miss Blythe—
said some pleasant things about you, too. See you
later."

By way of reply, Wayne, who was now quite
awake, slowly nodded his head. Then he crossed the
room again, and sitting on the edge of the bed for
some moments, stared wide-eyed at the door through
which his new friend had made his exit.

"And I'll bet," he mumbled, as he slowly got back
into bed and pulled the clothes up to his chin, "I'll

"Very nice girl, that Miss Blythe — said some pleasant things about you, too."

bet in those riding things that boy will look like the original fairy prince. Damn him!"

After breakfast Janet Hone and Wayne met on the hotel porch, as they usually met every morning.

"Strange stories," Janet began as she vaulted up on the railing—"strange tales I've been hearing of your new friend. Where does he think he is—Monte Carlo? But that's always the way—to whom it hath. I hear that he is very rich."

Wayne gazed up at the light, blue sky and smothered a yawn. "He certainly dresses well."

Miss Hone looked at Wayne and drew her thin, pretty lips into a straight line.

"Isn't that like a man? Dresses well, eh? Why, that boy rises as superior to clothes as clothes do to a lay figure in a tailor's window. He has all the courtesy and the chivalry of the old South. His voice is the most soothing thing I ever heard, and every look from those big eyes when he is dancing with you is like a caress."

"Wonderful, marvellous young man," Wayne said,

"especially if he can so easily affect you, Janet. Here he comes up the road now with Eleanor Blythe."

Blackwood helped the girl to dismount, and the two young people, flushed with their brisk ride, ran up the piazza steps.

"Isn't he splendid in his riding-clothes?" whispered Janet.

"Splendid," Wayne whispered with mock enthusiasm. "I said he'd look like a fairy prince in those togs."

"Whom did you say that to?" Janet asked.

"To myself. Do you think I'm doing press work for an Adonis like that?"

"Good-morning," Janet and Wayne called, and waved their hands to the young couple as they were hurrying by on their way to the dining-room.

"Oh, Wayne," Blackwood threw over his shoulder. "Won't you and Miss Hone dine with me to-night? I hear there's a farm near here where they have the most wonderful Virginia cooking."

Wayne smiled grimly and shook his head. "And now he's giving dinner-parties."

"And why not?" demanded Miss Hone.

244

Wayne smiled. "Why not, indeed?" he repeated.

From that morning Blackwood became an integral, even important, factor in the life of the Springs. His methods were conspicuous almost to the point of being ostentatious, but he entertained much and entertained well, and the stories of his exceptional winnings at the Meeting-Room were therefore forgiven. Besides, the rumor was generally current that he was rich in his own right. To the young people of his age he gave many dinners at Ridge Road Farm; he also gave a tea on the Casino lawn to a large party of old ladies; and he gave a hay-ride and picnic to the children.

"You see," he said to Wayne, by way of explanation, "the tea to the old ladies makes me more or less immune from porch gossip, for one afternoon, anyhow, and the party for the children squares me with the young married folks. The dinners at the farm are altogether different—they are for my own pleasure."

"Of course," Wayne said, and walked away, wondering what Blackwood's eventual pleasure would be.

THE DANCING MAN

The Southerner played neither golf nor tennis, but he was always wiling to follow a pretty girl over the links or to encourage her from the side-lines of a tennis-court. Perhaps he did not indulge in these sports because he was not apt in them, or it may have been that he was too firm a believer in the old life of the Springs, when riding and driving and dancing were the only legitimate pastimes of true gentlemen; but whatever the cause, he was, apparently, omnipresent and always content. He was not averse to a long tramp over the hills, and he and his horse, which he now hired by the week, were ready and eager for a riding-party at any time from sunrise until the moon hung high.

"And the wonderful thing to me about him," old Addicks said one day to Wayne, "is that with his multifarious social duties he always seems to have time to drop into a chair by an old lady or a spare half hour to dangle a kid on his knee, or tell a funny story to a group of old men. I tell you, Gordon County, Georgia, has given up its dead. That boy is his old man incarnate. I wonder sometimes what the lad's finish will be."

THE DANCING MAN

Wayne smiled and shook his head ominously.

"If I had to venture a guess," he said, "and this is not for publication I should say his finish would be very similar to that of a beautiful, round, iridescent bubble that floated up and up until it struck a perfectly hard ceiling."

Old Addicks smiled. "Perhaps," he said, "and yet sometimes as I watch him, I wonder if this particular bubble is not clever enough to dodge the ceiling. I think he'll surprise us all before the summer is over."

The three who saw him most intimately were Janet Hone, Eleanor Blythe and Arthur Wayne. Almost every evening they drove to Ridge Road Farm and dined together at the quaint little farm-house. Here it was that they told heir best stories, laughed over the gossip of the Springs, and, far from the wagging tongues of the hotel porches, had their simple pleasures in their own quiet way. It was not strange, under the circumstances, that the four should become fairly intimate friends in so short a space of time. There were moments when Wayne stopped to wonder if he had done well in adopting Blackwood

as a protegè and practically standing sponsor for
him. After all, he had but loaned him some clothes
and a few dollars for poker money, and given him
credit for a fortune he did not possess; he would have
done that for almost any one. The trouble was that
Wayne was much the older of the two men, and
there was a general impression abroad that he had
known Blackwood always, and was, in a way, responsible for him, and Wayne had never done anything
to correct the impression. Several times he had considered telling Janet that Blackwood had come to
the Springs as a dancing-man and that the stories of
his wealth were mere fabrications—a sort of practical joke. But, after all, there was no disgrace in
being a dancing-man, and Blackwood's money affairs
could in no way affect Janet, as she had much more
money in her own right than she really needed. Besides, she was quite capable of taking care of herself. Wayne's own mild efforts at love-making, during several summers, had convinced him that the
girl had most excellent control over her emotions.
Any further doubts which he might have had as to
his relations toward Blackwood were also dispelled

by the fact that of the two girls the young Southerner seemed to prefer Eleanor Blythe; that is, if he ever showed signs of preference for any one.

They had all dined together at the farm one night, and Miss Blythe and Blackwood had wandered off toward the little stream that ran at the foot of the lawn, and left Janet and Wayne sitting on the porch. Wayne nodded toward the disappearing figures.

"What do you really think?" he asked.

The girl looked at him for some moments and then shrugged her shoulders.

"Oh, that's all right," she said; "that is, if they are both as well off in this world's goods as they appear to be. Blackwood, with money, is a delight—he's the sort of man any woman could be foolish about; but without money I imagine he would be a different proposition altogether. He likes the good things of life and his nerves need plenty of good sky and sunshine. I'm afraid his joyous nature would wilt if it rained too hard and too long."

"Perhaps," Wayne said; "but she has money— that is, she has all the appearances of it."

249

"Yes, to you, of course, but men are not always the best judges of appearances so far as women are concerned—especially at a Southern summer resort. I don't know anything about Eleanor except that she seems to be a very fine sort of a person, and I'm sure she wouldn't wilt however hard it might rain; but if you knew as much of some of these girls as I do you would be sorry. Now, mind you, I know very little of——"

"Sorry," Wayne interrupted. "Sorry they are not rich, or because there are not men enough to go around?"

"No, I'm sorry because some of them take men too seriously, and that includes their mothers, too. A girl should play a bout with a man because he interests or amuses her—not because he is a human being in trousers. Many of these girls here and their mothers and their mothers before them got their relative values mixed a long time ago—at least from my point of view.'

"According to the general scheme of things," Wayne suggested, "men have always been a necessary evil."

Janet drew her lips into a straight line and clasped her hands back of her head.

"I'm afraid you don't quite understand," she said. "You see nothing but a smiling face and a pretty muslin dress. You don't know what privation some of the families from those little Southern towns suffer to give the daughter a month at 'The Springs.' Mind you, I am speaking of some, not all of them. The father works all winter, and the mother sews on her daughter's dresses, and they both ward off the young man around the corner. And then when summer rolls around father keeps on working and mother brings the girl to the Springs looking for the Fairy Prince. Your modern little Diana, in a pretty shirt-waist and a dimity skirt, goes out to hunt the Prince while mother sits on the hotel porch or on one of the fringe of chairs around the ballroom and cheers on the chase. It's not a pretty sight, and it puts the little Diana and the Fairy Prince in a position which neither of them usually cares much about or deserves."

"And afterward?" Wayne asked.

Janet unlaced her fingers from behind her head,

stood up and smoothed the creases out of her duck skirt. "Afterward," she repeated, "they make the best wives and mothers in the world—that is, up to the time when they bring their own daughters to the Springs looking for the new generation of fairy princes. They play the marriage game mighty well down here—that is, the serious end of it—I only object to the way they first catch the hare."

There was a long silence, while Wayne lit a cigar and blew clouds of gray smoke up to the rafters of the porch, and Janet leaned against one of the round white pillars and looked out idly on the starlit sky and at the jagged line of trees that fringed the little stream at the foot of the lawn.

"Ah," she said at last, "here comes the fairy prince."

Wayne chuckled to himself. "Is Blackwood a real fairy prince?" he asked.

Janet looked down at him and nodded her pretty head. "Yes," she said, "he's a pretty fair fairy prince—wonderful under a hot sun or a full moon, and that is as much as we can ask of most men. After all, you are very much like the little figures in the weather-box. Some come out in good weather and some in bad, but never both at the same time."

"And Miss Blythe," Wayne asked—"is she in the Diana class?"

Janet Hone smiled. "I don't know, and I don't suppose I would tell you if I did. I was talking of types—not individuals. At least, this one hides her arrows—perhaps she has been shooting at Blackwood in the dark."

For the first time, Wayne did not enjoy the drive back to the Springs—in fact, for the greater part of the time he was as unconscious of the high hills that lined the narrow gap through which the road led as he was of Janet Hone who sat beside him. His thoughts were all of the girl and of the man directly in front of him. Suppose that, after all, she was such a girl as Janet had described, and that she believed, as he himself had led the others to believe, that Blackwood was rich and was everything that he probably was not. Supposing that Blackwood, believing that Eleanor had money, had already asked her to marry him, and supposing that her mother, sharing the belief in Blackwood, had induced her to accept him. Suppose that of her own accord she had promised to marry him—suppose she loved him. And it was all his own fault—it was he who had deceived Eleanor Blythe about Blackwood, as he had every one else, and now it seemed possible that this young girl was to bear the brunt of his foolish practical joke.

For the next few days the four friends played about together as they had done for the past two weeks, with perhaps the difference that they saw a little more of each other and less of the other visitors at the Springs. Exactly how matters stood between Eleanor Blythe and Blackwood, Wayne could only speculate, for Janet absolutely refused to speak further on the subject, and it was impossible to tell anything from the Southerner himself, because his manner was just as devoted to one girl as to the other—in fact, as it was to every woman with whom he came in contact.

They had continued to take long walks together and to drive together, and on the third day they dined together again at the Ridge Road Farm. On their return they had separated at the hotel steps, and

254

THE DANCING MAN

Blackwood had taken Miss Blythe to her cottage. Wayne and Janet walked up the long porch to the hotel door, where for some time they stood discussing the plans for the next day. As Wayne left her and started for his own cottage, he found Addicks leaning against the balustrade of the porch.

"Don't be in a hurry," the old man called to him. "You're so busy of late that you have forgotten your former friends altogether. Stop a bit; it's too nice a night to go to bed. Besides, I wanted to tell you a story."

"What kind of a story?" Wayne asked.

"Well, it's only a sort of reminiscence. I was watching your friend Blackwood from my dark corner just now and I was thinking how very, very like he was to his father and how curiously often history repeated itself—especially down here, where I don't think people change as much as they do in the North. And somehow this thought got mixed up with our talk of the other day as to just what young Blackwood's finish would be after his meteoric career at the Springs."

Wayne nodded. "I've wondered about that,

too," he said—"wondered about it a good deal of late."

"I was watching you all," Addicks continued, "as you drove up the road and said good-night— watching young people is about all that an old man can do for active amusement. I noticed Blackwood took that pretty Miss Blythe to her cottage and afterward he came back here. Just below where I was standing he met Wilson, the livery-stable man, and I heard him order a trap for half-past six to-morrow morning. He said that he must have a good horse because he wanted to drive to Pine Valley. I didn't want to listen, but from where I stood it was impossible not to hear what he said."

"I wouldn't worry over it if I were you," Wayne said, smiling. "What was your story about?"

"I wasn't really worrying, and I was just coming to the story." The old man pointed with his cane across the dark lawn. "Do you see that light in the last room of Claiborne Circle?"

Wayne nodded.

"That was my room in the old days. I had had a bad time of it one night and I got up about six o'clock in the morning and went out on the porch to get some fresh air in my lungs. The sun wasn't over the mountains yet and it was quite gray and misty, but down the road there I saw Jack Blackwood, this boy's father, sitting in a buggy. He was flecking flies off the horse, just as unconcerned as you and I are now, but I knew that something was up sure, for that was no hour for Jack to go buggy-riding. And then the door of the Rambler Cottage opened a bit and out came Mary Bent. She was the prettiest thing you ever saw—just like some dainty white flower—and when she saw Jack she smiled and threw him a kiss and fluttered down the steps and along the path, more as if she were flying than running to him. I never was a man of action, so I went back to my room and waited till I heard the wheels of the buggy pass. I guess there wasn't much I could have done anyhow. She was crazy about him the first time she saw him, but we didn't quite believe it —because we didn't want to, I suppose."

The old man puckered his lips and drew his white shaggy eyebrows together until they almost met, and for some moments both men remained silent, looking across the deserted stretches of lawn and beyond to the distant hills.

"It was about ten o'clock that morning when they drove up to the hotel, and the sun was shining, I remember, and everybody on the porch lined up at the railing because it was a curious time for any one to be coming in. I think Mary had been crying, at least it looked as if she had, and Jack was a little glum himself, for he hadn't done much to be proud of. He tossed the reins to one of the boys, and then they got out and came up the steps arm-in-arm and walked straight up to Mrs. Bent and told her how they had gone to Pine Valley, just over the state border, and had been married."

"And then?" Wayne asked.

"Oh, I don't know," the old man sighed. "Jack took her back to Sackett, and I can't imagine that much good ever came of it—except, perhaps, this boy. A run-down family estate at Sackett, as it was in those days, and especially with Jack Blackwood, is hardly the life most of us would choose, and yet she was a woman in ten thousand. But Jack had a wonderful way with the women."

258

THE DANCING MAN

The old man threw away his cigar, yawned, and started down the porch.

"Good-night," he called over his shoulder. "I hope I didn't bore you. Good-night."

For a few moments Wayne remained leaning against the balustrade. Then he went into the hotel office, which, with the exception of an old colored servant who was cleaning the place, was quite deserted. Going to the desk, he scribbled a note and gave it to the old man to take to Eleanor Blythe. A few minutes later he left the hotel, walked slowly along the driveway, and then turned down the path that led past the rear of the Blythes' cottage. He found Eleanor waiting for him in the shadow of the screen of vines that trailed over the little porch.

"I'm so glad you could let me see you," he said.

The girl's white lips broke into a cheerless little smile and for a moment she laid her cold hand in the strong, firm one held out to her.

"I'm afraid it's very late," she whispered. "I don't want to disturb mother, and then you know how people talk."

259

"That's all right," Wayne said, "I'll talk very low. But I must speak to you to-night."

"Wouldn't to-morrow do?"

"It certainly would not."

The girl shrugged her shoulders, sat down on the top step, and with her elbows on her knees, rested her chin between her palms. Wayne sat at her feet, his back against the porch railing, and for some moments looked up frankly at the pale pretty face.

"Do you know much about Blackwood?" he began.

Miss Blythe turned her eyes slowly from the moon-lit path at her feet to those of the man and shook her head.

"No," she said, "not very much. Just as you know him, I imagine. As every one——"

"That's just it," Wayne interrupted. "That's just why I am here—I don't think you know him as I do."

The girl drew her pretty curved lips into a straight line and with wrinkled brow looked at him questioningly.

"I'm afraid I don't quite understand," she said.

"Why should you care what I know about Black-wood?"

"Because I'm entirely responsible for the very false position he just now happens to occupy. I'm not given to telling women all I know about men, but in this particular case I've got to talk, and I think that you had better listen."

Again the girl shrugged her shoulders and turned her eyes back to the path.

"Several weeks ago," Wayne went on, "when Blackwood first came to the Springs, he had just enough money to stay here for a fortnight at the rate they give dancing men."

"Have you anything against dancing men getting special rates?" the girl asked. "It's a very old custom down here—lots of men I know do it."

"I certainly have no objection to a man getting the best rates he can," Wayne continued unmoved, "but I have an objection to a man pretending to be something he is not. I loaned Blackwood every stitch he has worn at the Springs, and I loaned him the money with which he has made his winnings at the Meeting-Room. It was I who started the report as to his solid wealth, and so far as I know he has done nothing to correct that report. It was begun as a sort of practical joke and I don't propose to have it end in a tragedy—that is, if I can help it. You may find Blackwood the most charming of men. That is none of my affair—but I think it is my affair to tell you that all the money he has spent here he has made at cards since he came, and the fortune you have heard about does not exist. So far as Blackwood's life at the Springs is concerned, it is nothing more or less than a plain and apparently very successful case of bluff. I think that's all I wanted to say."

Wayne started to rise, but the girl put out her hand.

"Don't go yet," she said; "that is, if you can wait a few minutes longer. Mother is probably awake by this time, and I've no doubt my reputation is already gone for talking with you here at all at this hour."

Wayne settled back in his former position and Miss Blythe leaned against the wall of the cottage, and having clasped her hands behind the mass of curls stared up for some moments at the roof of the little porch. It was she who at last broke the silence.

THE DANCING MAN

"As a matter of fact," she began, "I do not know so very much more of your life than I do of Blackwood's, and yet I should imagine that you have never really seriously wanted for anything in this world that you couldn't have. I should judge this from what I have heard from your friends who know you in the North and from the way that we have known you here. I don't remember when I have ever met a man who was more thoughtful and considerate of women than you are, and now it seems your charity has extended to poor dear Blackwood. But I wonder how it would have been with you if you were really poor and had spent your life on a little God-forsaken farm in the mountains. I wonder if you, too, would not have been glad to parade in good clothes and play at being rich for just a few weeks. There is nothing of a bluff about you. It seems to me that you are very sincere and genuine, and now that we are telling only truths, I don't mind saying that I like you very much—more than you probably have any idea of. But, after all, you have never had any temptations to be a bluff. I wonder how it would have been with you if you had been brought up—as Blackwood probably was, and I surely was—in a small Southern town, starved in body and soul?"

Wayne looked curiously into the girl's face, but she did not see him for she was still looking up into the rafters of the porch.

"I think I'll tell you about my own case," she went on, speaking very slowly, "because perhaps it will make you a little more charitable, although you will probably hate me for it, and I don't like to think of your doing that. But in a few days now every one will know the story, and I think—at least that is the way I feel to-night—that I would rather tell you myself." She looked down at him and let her hands fall idly in her lap. "You don't mind staying a little while longer?"

By way of answer, he reached out and took one of her hands in his, and she let it lay there when she began speaking again.

"About three years ago my father died, and at that time he was supposed to be quite a rich man— that is, rich for a small town. Certainly we all had everything we could want, and even if the life was very narrow, I was only a girl, and mother and I had already begun to make plans about going abroad, and travelling about in this country, too. I don't know a great deal about business, but I imagine father was one of those men who are so honest themselves that they believe every one else to be honest as well. It seems he had lost a lot of money not long before he died, and so mother and I were left with really almost nothing, although no one but Mr. Lewis, who was father's lawyer, and we knew it. For more than two years we lived on very quietly, and then one day last winter we had a long talk with Mr. Lewis, and we found that we had just five thousand dollars in the whole world—nothing else— just five thousand dollars between us and absolute poverty. Of course we might have made this last some time, but I guess mother and I had the gambling spirit in us, too, so after we had talked it over a great many times, we decided to form a sort of stock company. The stock was the five thousand dollars, and mother was what, I think, you would call the promoter, and I was the asset. That was a foolish idea, wasn't it?"

Wayne looked evenly into the girl's eyes and shook

his head. "I don't know," he said. "Was it a foolish idea?"

"It was a bad business idea," she went on, "because our working capital is gone and the asset proved to be altogether worthless. I guess the market was overcrowded. We opened the campaign in Baltimore, but the game was too big for us there, and the few people we knew didn't seem to care about our little enterprise, and so we moved on to Richmond. They certainly were sweet to us in Richmond, but all the eligible men apparently had a sort of permanent understanding with the girl around the corner. We did the Annapolis graduation and the University of Virginia Commencement, but at both places the men were all boys, and at Annapolis they all wanted to be naval heroes; and at Charlottesville the whole graduating class had decided not to marry until they were Henry Clays. It was very discouraging, so we took a short trip to Virginia Beach, and then—then we came here. It didn't really promise so very well, but the funds were getting a little low, and mother used to come here a long time ago, and she sort of wanted to get back again. It's won-

derful how people return to this place. I suppose
if I——"

The girl suddenly stopped, looked at Wayne, and
then turned her misty eyes out to the long stretches of
moonlit lawn. Her little fingers tightened about his big
hand, and thus for some moments they sat in silence.

"And now," she said with a little catch in her
voice, "you see the money is all gone and the company has failed and—and, well, it's all over. Do you
blame me—do you blame me very much? Just suppose you had a mother—I mean a mother that had
been like your mother who had had everything all
her life. I tell you there are lots of bluffs in this
world. Is it any worse than the rich girl in the North
who spends her father's money for a position or a
title? They buy—I sell—what's the difference?"

The girl drew away her hand and pressed it hard
against her cold forehead Wayne slowly got up and
stood looking down at her.

"I know a great ending to that story," he said,
and giving his hand to the girl, helped her to her
feet. "That is, it would be a great ending from my
way of looking at things. At six o'clock to-morrow

morning—not half-past six, mind you—I will be waiting in a runabout at the front door of your cottage. We can be at Pine Valley by eight, and the clergyman there will marry us, and we will be back here before ten."

The girl put out her hand and laid it on his shoulder, but he took it in his and kissed the tips of her fingers. "Please don't say anything now," he whispered—"please don't, because you're very tired. I'll look for your answer to-morrow morning. Don't forget, I'll be waiting for you at six."

It was just eight o'clock the following morning when Mr. and Mrs. Arthur Wayne stood on the clergyman's porch at Pine Valley and bade their new-found friends good-by. The reverend gentleman smiled because he considered that he had done a good deed and had been more than generously paid for it; his good wife smiled because she believed that it was about as good to be married as to be born a Carolinian; the two lady neighbors smiled because it had not often been their fate to act as witnesses to a marriage, and, at least for the moment, their importance would no doubt be considerably enhanced in the immediate neighborhood; Eleanor and Arthur Wayne smiled because of course the happiest moment in any man's and woman's life is when they first discover that they are really in love with each other. They shook hands several times all around, and then Wayne helped Mrs. Wayne into the runabout, and, still smiling, they started for home along the sunlit road. The air was filled with a wonderful golden haze, the fields that lay on either side sparkled with a million crystal dew-drops, and through the trees of the hills before them little fleecy clouds drifted slowly up to the turquoise sky.

"Are you happy, dear?" he whispered.

The girl threw up her chin and the word that she would have spoken died in her throat. With the back of her hand she brushed away the mist from her eyes and the other she laid in his free hand, and thus they drove on their way.

It was but a short time after this, at a sharp turning in the road, that Wayne pulled aside to let another trap pass. The eyes of the occupants of the two runabouts met at the same moment.

"Hello, Blackwood!" Wayne called as the horses were pulled to a standstill.

"Hello, yourself," Blackwood said, while Janet Hone and Eleanor beamed pleasantly at each other, and then at the two men.

"We're going to get married at Pine Valley," Blackwood said. "Wish you would come along as witnesses."

Wayne looked at Eleanor and shook his head. "I think not," he apologized. "Mrs. Wayne and I are pretty late as it is. Besides, you will find some most capable witnesses there already—that is, if you hurry up. Good-by—see you at the Springs."

They had gone but a short distance when Wayne heard the patter of footsteps behind them and pulled up his horse.

"Hello, Blackwood," he said, "what's the trouble?"

For a moment the Southerner leaned on the wheel of the runabout trying to recover his breath.

"It's like this, Arthur," he panted, "I forgot to bring a ring. Could you——?"

"Sure I could," Wayne said, and pulling off a seal ring dropped it in Blackwood's hand. "But, old man," he added, "please return it, because it's an heirloom, and it has been in the family a long, long time."

"That's funny," Blackwood said; "didn't any of your family ever meet a Blackwood?" And then he ran down the road still chuckling aloud.

"A funny boy," Eleanor said, as they once more started on their way.

Wayne glanced up curiously at the pretty face and then at the big straw hat that shaded it.

"He is a funny boy," he repeated. "I think I'll ask you a question, Eleanor."

"Why, yes, of course, dear," she said. "Is it a serious question?"

"Not at all serious. It really doesn't make any difference now—not a bit. But did Blackwood ever ask you to drive with him in the early morning—to Pine Valley, for instance?"

"Why, no," she laughed. "Such a funny question for you to ask! What could possibly make you think that he had ever asked me?"

Wayne smiled, and with the whip gently flicked a fly from the horse's neck.

THE DANCING MAN

"I really don't know," he said. "Except, I imagine that all true lovers are naturally jealous and suspicious—don't you?"

THE GREATEST OF THESE

THE GREATEST OF THESE

As he stepped off the train Crichton glanced up at the big black clock with the gold hands just as if he had been a commuter from Scarsdale or Mamaroneck. In reality it had been over two years since he had set foot in his native town, but his mind, like that of all good travellers, focussed itself unconsciously and immediately upon familiar places. It was already a quarter past three o'clock, so he hurried over to the telephone booths to call up Curtis before his friend should have left the little glass office down in Wall Street.

A quarter past three is usually a very busy moment in a broker's office, and Crichton was reminded of the fact by the snarl from the office boy who answered his call. Even Brooke Curtis himself spoke somewhat peremptorily until he quite understood who was at the other end of the wire. Then there came: "Well, well, well—that's fine. Arrived in Boston this morning, eh? You say you're at the

Grand Central. Well, check your stuff right out to the place and take the three-forty train. Try to make yourself comfortable, and I'll be out on the four-forty-five in time for a game of squash. Tell them you have come to stay—don't forget. Stay—sure. Headquarters while you are in this country. It's really great—you've saved my life—this town is dead in summer. I'll telephone them to meet you at the station. Good-by!"

An hour later Crichton was lounging in a deep leather chair in Curtis's billiard-room. He had changed to his flannels and was smoking and reading the time away until the master of the house should return and join him in a game of squash—preceded, of course, by the traditional walk through Curtis's beloved vegetable gardens and greenhouses. He dropped his book and blew a long, thin cloud of gray tobacco smoke into the yellow sunshine, which stretched an unbroken path from the open window to the great, empty hearth across the room. The whole place was filled with a golden haze, and through this and the gray smoke Crichton looked out of the broad window on the stretch of deep green

276

sward running down to the water and then beyond to the sheering walls of the Palisades.

The man smiled at the wonderful beauty of it all, and marvelled how anything could have remained so long unchanged. Since his college days, when he used to spend his summer vacations with Curtis, he had looked out on that same scene of green grass, and blue water, and gray rocks, and it was the one picture of America that he had always remembered on his travels in strange countries. It came to him at times when he was a little tired, mentally, or when he had been ill in a foreign land and with strange faces about him.

Ever since Brooke Curtis had first become master of Edgemere it had been an unwritten law that, during the summer months, no women folks, not even women servants, should ever enter this wing of the house. Curtis and his younger brother Ned had their rooms here, and so had Crichton, one story above them. On the ground floor was the billiard-room, and as there was no danger of feminine intrusion, Curtis and his men guests usually wandered about the whole wing in the most unconventional of summer garments. It so happened on this occasion that Crichton was in a fairly presentable condition, although he had already discarded his coat and tie and had rolled up his sleeves in anticipation of the coming contest at squash. When through half-closed eyes he first saw the tall figure with the flimsy white waist and the long, close-fitting duck-skirt, it seemed as if some fairy princess had risen from the lawn and was coming to waken him from his dream. And then, as he instinctively pulled himself out of the low chair, he became quite conscious that this was no fancy at all, but a very good-looking girl who was breaking in where she had no right to break in. She certainly was very good to look upon, at least so Crichton thought, as, unconscious of his presence, she came through the high French window, the sunlight falling on a mass of golden brown hair, and lighting up the clear skin, flushed after a long walk over country roads. It was, however, with a certain amount of unpreparedness, both as to his mental and physical attitude, that Crichton rose to receive his lady visitor.

At the sight of him she uttered a low cry of surprise and stepped back toward the window.

"It's all right. I assure you, it's all right," urged Crichton. "Just let me get into my coat and I'll introduce myself."

"It's all right if you don't get into your coat," the girl said. "It's rather becoming. Ned told me I must never come in here, but I was quite sure that no one was at home."

"Ned told you?" Crichton asked.

"Yes, I'm Miss Ferguson; Ned and I are stopping over at the Ellisons'."

"Delighted," and Crichton bowed. "I'm Jim Crichton—you may have heard—Brooke and I——"

"I'm afraid not," she interrupted and held out her hand as if Crichton had been her oldest man friend. "You see I've only joined the family very recently, and I really don't know any one in New York. I'm from the Golden West."

"Really," said Crichton, "and did I understand you to say that you had joined the family?"

"Oh, you don't know, then?" The suggestion of a blush heightened the girl's color.

"I'm afraid not," he answered. "I, too, have been away for some time."

"Well, you see," she said, "I'm engaged to Ned. Yes, I am, regularly engaged. Announced and everything. Would you like to see my ring?"

Miss Ferguson laid her hand in his, and Crichton examined with much solicitude a splendid cabochon ruby.

"Do you like it?" she asked.

"Perfect!" he said, and released her hand.

"That's what I tell Ned; it's quite perfect. It's really the only engagement ring I ever saw that wasn't tagged with an apology. Every girl friend I ever had when she showed her engagement ring said that it wasn't what Billy or Tommy or Harry really intended to give her, but just as he was going to buy it the market went up or went down, or a rich old aunt who ought to have died didn't. You know all the sentiment really went out of engagement rings with tam-o'-shanters and kissing games. What do you think of Ned, really? You must know him pretty well—you seem so much at home here."

Crichton started to pull down his sleeves.

"No," the girl said, "that's all right. Leave them up. I didn't mean that, really. Why don't you take

some Scotch? There it is back of you on the table—
club soda and everything. Please don't mind me.
Ned says I drive him to drink. Queer effect to have
on a man, no?" Crichton got up and moved in the
direction of the little table with the bottles and high
glasses and a big bowl of ice.

"To be quite candid," he said, "I don't think
that Ned is good enough for you. Ned's a nice, handsome lad, at least he used to be, but he's not in
your class at all."

"Now you're making fun of me. Don't think I
always talk so much as I have just now, because
I'm really rather a serious person. I was a little
nervous. You see it was against the rules to
come in here at all, but it was a short cut to the
library.'

"Where's Ned now?" Crichton asked.

"I left him on his way to the stables. There's
something the matter with his riding horse. How
long have you known him?"

"Always. You see I was a kid friend of Brooke's
even before we went to college together. Ned sort of
grew up at my knee."

Crichton poured out a drink and, carrying his glass, walked over to the empty hearth.

"It must be fun," said Miss Ferguson, "to go to college for four years with men one really cares for."

"Yes," said Crichton, "there were three of us. There were Brooke and Willie Sherman and myself. We were always together for those four years—four long, beautiful years, when we never knew a care or had a doubt that the world had been made for our especial benefit."

"And then——?"

"And then came the awakening—the *débâcle*. The winter after we had taken our degrees we learned of what very little account we really were. Curtis became an ununiformed messenger boy in his father's office by day and a cotillion leader by night; Willie Sherman conceived a lively up-to-date interest in people who had lived a few thousand years before and spent his livelong days digging up mounds where it seems they had carelessly left their bones and foolish trinkets."

"And what became of you?"

Crichton straightened up and looked fairly into her eyes. In his glance, it seemed to Miss Ferguson, there was a certain look of surprise and wonder that she really did not know what had become of him·

"I went to Paris," he said.

The girl smiled. "Ah, that wicked city."

"Yes, it is wicked, I suppose," he said, "for women and boys just out of college. They rob you women at the dressmakers' by day and the boys at the cafés and cabarets by night. Still, it's a well-lit city and it seems rather cheery after a few months in the desert, or a winter with the faded yellows and pinks of Spain and Italy. There is so much there for the old ones who have dug deeper than the veneer that the tourist loves. Why, Paris is as full of us dead ones as the catacombs of Saint Calixtus. I just came from there."

"How lonely the other dead ones must be," Miss Ferguson said. "What were they doing?"

"Oh, just about the same thing—watching the Seine boats and feeding the sparrows in the Bois and sharing the ignominy of Alsace-Lorraine by plastering her statue with tin wreaths."

"And the live ones?" she asked.

"*Le monde du sport?* Oh, they were beating each other's brains out at polo at Bagatelle and climbing up Montmartre every night to hear a man sing at a new cabaret. Rather amusing he was, too—sort of a Fragson chap. He really had one great song." Crichton walked over to the piano, carefully put down his cigarette and glass of Scotch, and ran his fingers lightly over the keys.

"Do you speak boulevardier French?"

The girl nodded. "Pretty well. Ned takes *La Vie Parisienne*, and a girl I know who lives over there sends me most of the café-concert songs. I send her the new coon songs—sort of musical exchange. Please go on." She put her elbows on the piano and rested her chin between the palms of her hands. Crichton swung the piano-stool half around toward the girl and partly sang and partly recited the song to her.

"My, but you do speak good French," said Miss Ferguson when Crichton had finished and had begun feeling his way through the introduction of another song. "That song is really quite wonderful, isn't it?

It's so direct and simple, and there is such a hopeless tragedy under the apparent humor of it all.
Who wrote it?"

"I don't know the gentleman's name. I imagine it
was the swan song of one of the dead ones. Probably wrote it on a marble table at a café, dressed in
a slouch hat, a black cape, and a flowing tie, and a
large glass of absinthe in front of him."

"And all Paris," she added, "is singing the story
of a man's life while the man is starving in a
garret?"

"Probably," said Crichton, "and no doubt we shall
learn later that he sold that very song for five francs,
while the publisher with his illegitimate proceeds
built a dirigible airship that was the talk of all Paris.
Did you ever hear that French song of the airship
and the automobile? No? Well, then, I'll sing it to
you, but in the absence of a chaperon I think we will
omit the last two verses."

When the song was finished Crichton got up and
bowed to the girl and waved his hand in the direction
of the piano-stool.

"My first number," she said, "is rather a showy

piece, even a little theatrical. It's called 'A Bark at Midnight.'"

Half an hour later Ned Curtis found his fiancée still at the piano and Crichton deep in an armchair sipping his Scotch and looking straight ahead at the girl's brown hair, which the soft rays of the dying sun streaked with gold. The two men shook hands warmly.

"Did you ever hear Miss Ferguson sing 'A Bark at Midnight'?" Crichton asked.

Curtis said that he really didn't know and left it to Miss Ferguson, but the girl, coloring a little, admitted that he had not, and continued to run her fingers lightly over the keyboard.

"I think it's the most wonderful thing I ever heard," Crichton said. "I really believe that she would have played it the third time for me if you hadn't interrupted."

And then Brooke Curtis, the master of the house, came hurrying in with a very boisterous welcome, and the song and even Miss Ferguson and her fiancé were forgotten in the greeting of the two old friends.

"Come on," said Curtis; "we'll take a walk around the grounds. I want to hear all about yourself, and these two young lovers would be in the way."

"Good-by, Mr. Crichton," said Miss Ferguson; "we won't be here when you return. Thank you so much for the songs. I wish you would send me the one the Montmartre poet wrote if you can get it for me. Good-by."

They shook hands and then Crichton and Curtis, arm-in-arm, went out and left Miss Ferguson and Ned together. The young man crossed the room and leaned over the deep lounging chair in which she sat. Mechanically she raised her hand, which he took in both of his, and, raising it to his lips, lightly kissed the tips of her fingers. The girl's eyes followed the figures of the two men crossing the lawn.

"What an unusual person your friend Crichton is," she said. "How is it that I never heard you speak of him before?"

The young man, still holding her hand, sat on the broad arm of the chair. "I don't know," he said, "except that he has always been Brooke's particular friend. He is a good deal older than I am, but I rather thought pretty much every one had at least heard of Jim Crichton."

"What would one hear?' she asked. "Good things?"

The young man got up and crossing to the table slowly began to prepare himself a drink. "Yes and —no," he said. "He is and always was one of the finest men God ever made, but Jim made one mistake."

"What kind of mistake?" she asked. "It must have been very serious.'

"It was," he said, "one of the kind people never forget, though in a way they forgive. I might as well tell you, because somebody else will sooner or later, and I'll tell you the true story."

The girl settled deeper in the low chair, her eyes still following the two men, who, far across the lawn, had stopped to examine a wall covered with old English ivy.

"When Crichton had finished college," he began, "he went over to Paris and settled down. One way and another he spent a good deal of money, at least

288

his father thought so, although the old man was
very rich. However, for a long time he kept on send-
ing Jim remittances far beyond his allowance, but
he didn't fail to tell him what he thought of his
extravagance. Finally, Jim got in with a pretty quick
crowd and he used to play poker and baccarat with
them at one of the clubs. Well, one morning he woke
up and found himself very much in debt. The men
whom he owed weren't the kind he could ask for
time, and it was just a plain case of pay. He cabled
his father exactly how things stood, and in a few
hours he got a pretty rough answer, absolutely refusing the money and telling him he would have to
live thereafter on his regular income. Of course, Jim
had to have the money, but the old man's wire was
what did the business. I honestly believe, just out
of spite and to show his father that he couldn't down
him he signed a check with the old man's name for
twice the amount he had asked for. The rest was easy,
because the people at the bank knew Jim and knew
his father was good for any amount. But when the
check reached New York the old man denied it. I
suppose it was because he loved Jim better than

anything else in the world, and because he had done everything he could for him all his life, that he lost his head completely and denounced Jim as a forger all over his old office. Half an hour later he tried to deny everything he had said and insisted the check was all right, but it was too late. Every clerk in the place hurried uptown and told the story at some tea or dinner or club, and, although they kept the story out of the papers, it was all over with Jim."

"And then?" asked the girl.

"Oh, then? Well, Jim came home and the two of them started in to spend years trying to undo the harm they had both done in a moment of anger. It almost killed the old man, and Jim took him from one health resort to another, trying all kinds of cures, but there was no cure for that kind of trouble. The old man died in his arms, asking the boy's forgiveness with his last breath. I guess Jim would have been willing to quit then too, but he had the young machinery the old man lacked, and so he kept on going."

"And some of him lived, but the most of him died," Miss Ferguson interrupted.

"No, hardly that. As a matter of fact, Jim never was any good until he signed that check. He was a crazy, wild kid before that, but the trouble made a man of him absolutely. He couldn't turn to individuals any more, except to a few men like Brooke who loved him better than anybody in the world, because he knew they knew the story, and that it was always being told behind his back—just as I am telling it to you. So for lack of individual friends he made a friend of the whole world. He devoted himself to ideas and places and books and races of people. There is hardly a settlement where any white man has been that he doesn't know and know well, and I think he has read more, and more intelligently, than any one I ever heard of. Of course, the tragic part of it all is that Jim is at heart terribly social; he has the heart of a woman and he loves his kind more than any man I know. But instead of friends made of flesh and blood, he has to shut himself up in his library with only his books about him, or go out and look for companionship in some South African forest or along the rocks of some God-forsaken coast where white people don't even get shipwrecked."

"But he told me he often went to Paris," the girl interrupted.

"Oh, yes, he does. He slips back there just as he does over here sometimes. But it doesn't last. He can't go to the houses of the only kind of people he wants to know, or he can't be a member of a decent club. You would have hard work to find any individual who says he does not feel about Jim Crichton just as Brooke or I feel, but there is always that intangible force fighting against him. He is the very best in the world, but the world hasn't forgotten and never will forget that he once forged a miserable bit of paper. Now, tha 's Crichton's story, and I don't know what that song of yours is about that you sang to him, called 'A Bark at Midnight,' but, judging from the title, I'm not surprised that it interested him.'

Miss Ferguson got up and crossed the room to the broad window which looked out on the river, turned pink and gray in the 'ast rays of the setting sun.

"It's not a very happy story," she said. "And yet somehow it seems as long as his father forgave him the rest of the world might forget. Was there no practical way for him to get back? Couldn't Brooke, for instance, or you?"

Ned shook his head. "I don't think so," he said, "because if there had been any way Brooke would have discovered it long ago. I always had a theory that a woman could have done it. If he had married a girl of sufficient position and strength, I think she might have won back his place for him."

"And no woman ever loved him enough for that?"

"I suppose not," he said. "That is, no woman he cared for. It would be asking a good deal of a girl to share that kind of a life, and, besides, most men would rather drown than be thrown a life-preserver by a woman."

"And yet," answered Miss Ferguson, "the world is really very full of charity."

"In a way it is, but I think most people feel a good deal about it as they do about their securities; they prefer to put their investments in several baskets. It would take a lot of nerve for a woman to constitute Jim Crichton her favorite charity."

"I wonder," said the girl. "Ring for the cart,

won't you, Ned? It's time we were starting for the Ellisons'."

A few minutes later Crichton and Curtis stopped in their walk through the formal gardens long enough to wave to the young people who passed them on their way out of the grounds.

"Lucky boy, Ned, I must say, even if he is my own brother," said Curtis. "She'll make a wonderfully fine woman."

"Wonderful," Crichton added. "It was such fun to talk to a girl like that even for half an hour. I mean a girl who didn't know and just met you on your own."

Crichton stooped and kicked at a weed which the gardener had overlooked. "Do you suppose she knows now?" he asked.

Curtis put his arm through Crichton's and turned him in the opposite direction from the road down which the cart was fast disappearing.

"Dear old Jim" he said, "I suppose she does by now."

Crichton's stay in America was very short. He decided quite suddenly one day that he must return to the Far East. A letter from Paris ten days later to Brooke Curtis, and then he disappeared entirely. Summer passed and winter and summer again, and then one day, late in November, he turned up once more in New York. He went to his hotel and asked for a letter which was awaiting his arrival. Once in his room he tore off the envelope and reread the short note many times. This was all that it said:

DEAR MR. CRICHTON:—I shall be glad to see you any afternoon after five, as I am nearly always at home then to give my friends a cup of tea. It is good to know that you are about starting in this direction.

Indeed, I have often thought of the day I broke into the billiard-room and insisted on singing to you.

Sincerely yours,

MARGARET FERGUSON.

Late that afternoon he was standing in front of the fire in the drawing-room of the Ferguson home, and Miss Ferguson was sitting behind the teacups, looking, at least so Crichton thought, much more beautiful than she had looked that day he had first met her almost two years before.

"But this time," she said, "you have come to stay for a long visit?"

Crichton looked down into his teacup and smiled. "I fear not," he said. 'I am going away very soon."

"You're so disappointing. Can't you possibly stand us for a few weeks? Where are you going this time?"

"I haven't an idea," he said, "not the faintest, believe me."

"That's even less complimentary to us. What does Brooke say to this plan?"

"I haven't seen Brooke yet. You know I only arrived this afternoon. I wanted to see you first; in fact, it was to see you that I came back to this country. Not that I don't want to see Brooke, bless his soul, but——"

"You wanted to see me?" the girl interrupted him. "Me?"

The light from the fire shone full upon her face, and Crichton noticed that her color was very high and that her eyes seemed to avoid his.

"Yes," he repeated, clasping his hands behind him, "to see you and to ask you a favor. I am not

going to ask it because I think you owe me anything
or because I can ever possibly repay you, because
I can't. It's a favor you would do for an utter stranger,
because I think you are naturally charitable and because it really doesn't amount to much anyhow—at
least to you."

"You really are most mysterious," she said.
Crichton noticed that the color had left her face and
that she was smiling up at him quite pleasantly,
and so he smiled back at her.

"It really isn't very amusing, as a matter of fact.
It happened about this way. You remember that
very soon after I first met you two years ago I went
abroad?"

The girl nodded.

"My inclination was to think about you a great
deal, but I did my best not to do so. You see you
were engaged then to Ned, and for that and for other
reasons I tried to keep my mind on other people and
other things. And then one day, when I was down on
the west coast of Africa, I got a letter from a man
who writes me sometimes and he told me that you
were not engaged any more. So you see there was no

particular reason why I should not think of you all I wanted to, was there?"

Crichton hesitated, but Miss Ferguson did not notice him. She was looking into the fire, her chin resting between the palms of her hands.

"And soon after that," he continued, "I booked back to civilization, and when I reached Paris I got some very important news."

"Good news?" she asked without looking up.

Crichton shook his head. "I imagine most people would call it bad news," he said, "and I do, too, in a way. It seemed I had taken some sort of fever on the trip, and that had rather complicated matters in my system. I went to see a lot of doctors, and it was quite wonderful how they all agreed about me—one of them was quite hopeful. He said I might live a couple of months, but the best the rest could do was thirty days."

Her chin still resting in her hands, the girl slowly turned her eyes to his. She looked at him slowly from his head to his feet, as if she were trying to verify his words.

"I can't quite believe you," she said. "You don't

look like a dying man, and you certainly don't talk like one."

"If I should step into the firelight," he said, "I should certainly look like a man, with not even thirty days ahead of him; and as for the manner of my speech, it seems to me that my way is the only sane way to talk about it. It's wonderful how a big piece of news really affects one. The first doctor who told me was an old fellow in a frock coat and a Legion d'Honneur button, and his silk hat was on the desk in front of him in his office. I think he must have had an engagement for lunch, for he was forever glancing at his hat, and when he told me about how things stood he grabbed his hat and hurried out of the office ahead of me."

"And then?" asked Miss Ferguson.

"Then—oh—then? I went out, too, although rather slowly. It was a wonderful morning, just like spring, and I walked over to Laurent's and had lunch in the glass room. I was trying all the time to think just about how long it took thirty days to pass, and the only thing I could judge by was the monthly bills, and that made the time seem very short, because it always seemed to me that monthly bills come in at least twice a week. I had a very good lunch and enjoyed it, too, just like the men you read about in the papers the morning they are going to be hanged. And I sat some time smoking—long after the other people had left the place. Did you ever read that people who are drowning think of all their past sins?"

The girl nodded and leaned back in her chair, looking full into the shadowed face of the man silhouetted against the fire in the broad hearth.

"Well, do you know it never occurred to me to think of one single sin? I thought of all the happy hours I had ever spent. There were certain people and certain places and certain things that it just seemed as if I had to see before I quit. But, Lord, it was absolutely impossible. One of them, for instance, was a little stretch of beach on an island I always say I discovered in he South Pacific. At sunset the water is pink as coral and it runs up on the pebbles, and the stones look like great white pearls —it's quite wonderful. I have spent a great many happy days there. Another was a native girl I used to know in a little town just beyond Misda in Tripoli. She was very sweet and good to me once when I was sick, and I think she would really have been willing to marry me, too. She had a smile that I have travelled a great many miles to see several times, and— and there was a sheen to her copper skin. And then of course there were certain theatres in London and Paris, and there was a path in the Cascine at Florence I wanted to see again very much. The trees grow over it and after a shower, when the sun breaks out and shines through, the dripping leaves glisten like beautifully polished silver against the patches of gold sunshine. There were two or three Russian dishes I wanted to eat again, too, and I should have liked to hear that Hungarian band at Budapest. You know I never could understand good music. There is a place on Rhode Island where I should like to go back to. It's a queer, old-fashioned little place by the water, and I don't suppose it really means anything to most people, but I spent my summers there as a kid, and I like to go back and wander along the hard beach, and take long walks through the pines where we used to play at

Indian massacres. It's a nice old place, and all the distances seem so absurdly short compared to the old days, but it's terribly filled with ghosts—little ghosts of laughing children.

"There were lots of other things I wanted to do and see, but of course I couldn't run all over the world in thirty days very well, could I? I worked it out pretty well that day at Laurent's, and I argued and fought it out with myself for a long time. But gracious! I knew all the time what I wanted to do and what I was going to do, and that was to come back and see you and perhaps ask you to sing for me again."

As Crichton finished the girl looked up at him questioningly, but the man's face was still in the shadow.

"There is no hope?" she asked. "Doctors have given up many men for dead years and years ago and the men are alive to-day. We all know of such cases."

Crichton shook his head. "I'm afraid I'm not one of them," he said. "A month is the most I could have, and I had to beg for that. Just think, only a month

302

left of the sunshine and the sweetness of life. And I tell you it is sweet, Miss Ferguson, and it is fine and good—even if there are fogs, we learn in time that at some old place there is always a sun shining back of them."

"But it is a long while before the sun breaks through sometimes," she said. "I don't know just what to say to you, Mr. Crichton, because I really don't know you at all, and yet I feel that I never knew any one quite so well. I didn't break with Ned on account of you, but I did do it on account of your type, or rather on account of his. He was a good, sweet soul, but he was just like the rest of them here —the men, and the women too, for that matter are pretty much all made in the same mould. I have to go back to my father's ranch three months every year to keep near the earth and see all of the sky at once. You were different, and I wanted to know you very, very much. I was going to write you to come and see me in town before you sailed, and then——"

"And then?" he asked.

"Then? Well, why not? It can't make any difference now."

"None."

"I didn't send for you because I thought I cared too much."

"But you knew you were not going to marry Curtis?"

"Yes," she said, "I knew that from the first day."

"Then there must have been another reason?"

The girl nodded up at the dark figure. "Yes, there was another reason."

"Not the old reason—the reason of every dull fool that sits in a club window, the reason why every débutante is told to keep away from me?"

Miss Ferguson nodded.

Crichton, still standing with his back to the fire, clasped his hands behind him and slowly laced and unlaced his fingers.

"I judged," he said, "from what I saw of you before that above all you were charitable. I am sorry that I could not have gone away still thinking so."

"Charity?" she asked. "Do you call that charity? I mean the kind of charity that begins at home. It mayn't have been charitable to you or to me, but

304

the world wasn't made for you and me. We might as well try to dam a flood as to hold back what the world wants to think of us. And don't forget that the world isn't going to stop with us, any more than it began with us. Is it charity to cut the albatross from your own neck and tie it about another's?"

"And yet," the man interrupted, "our happiness would have made up for much. I don't pretend to be unselfish—the Lord knows I have suffered enough to want a little pleasure and peace before I die."

"I know," she said, "I know all of that. I know that we could have been happy, because we could have been content with each other and we could have gone away. But how do we know that those who came after us would have the strength to take up the burden? Do you know that they would have been satisfied, as you and I could have been, with only each other—happy with the heat of the sun over our heads and the smell of the ground under our feet? Do you know that those who might follow us would not choose to live with their kind, and do you know that they would be brave enough to hold up their heads in the crowded places?" The girl rose from her chair and, laying her hand on Crichton's shoulder, half turned him about, so that the red glare from the fire shone fairly in his face.

"I know it doesn't make very much difference now," she went on, "but I have told you what my own mother will never know. Is there anything else I can tell you before you go?"

The man and the girl stood for a moment looking into each other's eyes, and then Crichton shrugged his shoulders very slightly and smiled pleasantly into her face. It was a smile such as he might have vouchsafed a wayward child. He took the hand, which still rested on his shoulder, in both of his, and gently touched the tips of her fingers with his lips.

"There is nothing else," he said, "except to say good-by."

"Good-by," she whispered, "and God help you."

Crichton hailed a passing hansom and took his place in the long row of carriages moving slowly down the avenue. He glanced up with half-closed eyes at the many changes which had taken place since his last visit; narrow towering hotels and broad square banks had apparently grown up overnight, and the brownstone houses of the friends of the early days had been turned into decks of shop windows. But of the crowds on the sidewalks, the faces of the men and women in the passing carriages, he saw nothing—his thoughts were still of the firelit room he had just left and the girl who had told him "good-by." When he reached the hotel he found his servant waiting for him in his room.

"We are going to take a long trip this time, Lawrence," he said. "I don't want to reach Paris before the late spring or early summer, so I think we had better go by way of Yokohama. Find out, to-night if possible, when the next boat leaves 'Frisco."

THE EXECUTORS

THE EXECUTORS

SINCE the announcement of his engagement to Helen Trask, Wallace Stillwell Hamilton, or "Wallie" Hamilton as he was affectionately, and almost universally known, had become little better than a stranger to his numerous friends in town. Almost without exception, now, the late afternoon found him on his way from his office to the Grand Central Station, and his recent y acquired knowledge of "expresses" and "locals" between Rye and Forty-second Street was worthy of the oldest commuter. On rare occasions he made his mother very happy by dining with her at her home in the country and going over later to the Trasks, but more often he dined and spent the evening with Miss Trask, and on such occasions Mrs. Hamilton was rewarded only by a fleeting glimpse of her son on his arrival from town and a hearty kiss just before he turned in for the night. "Wallie" Hamilton had always been accounted a good son and now he was cheerfully admitted to be the true type of the perfect lover and husband-elect, and this, in spite of the fact that he and Helen Trask had been neighbors and playfellows as far back as either of them could remember anything.

Neglectful as he may have been of his other friends and acquaintances in town, Hamilton's engagement seemed only to have brought him the nearer to his most intimate friend—Lloyd Druce. The two had grown up together as boys, gone to the same preparatory school, graduated at the same university, and later, now more like brothers than friends, had returned to New York to work as well as play together. Formerly, when neither of them had been dining out, they had generally spent their evenings together at their club, or more often at the theatre, but now, on the rare occasions when Hamilton remained in town, the two men dined quietly at some restaurant and afterward went to Hamilton's apartment, where they filled the cosey sitting-room with slowly drifting gray clouds of tobacco smoke and talked a little of the days to come and a great deal of those that had gone.

THE EXECUTORS

The wedding was but a week distant, the details had all been arranged, the gifts, for the most part, had been received and acknowledged, and for the last time Hamilton was spending the night in town as a bachelor. He and Druce had dined late, and now Hamilton was sitting before his desk in the little study, and his friend was stretched out in a deep leather chair before the open hearth. The two young men had talked but little, and during a long silence, Hamilton opened a small drawer of the desk, fumbled among some papers, and took out a silver key ring from which there was suspended a single key. From the bunch of keys, which he always carried, he took another key and twisted it on to the silver ring. Then he swung his chair around so that he could see his friend.

"Lloyd," he said, "the lease of these rooms doesn't run out until May, and I don't want to sublet them. They're no good for Helen and me, so I think I will give you these duplicate keys. It might amuse you to run in here once in a while to borrow a book or—or just for old-time's sake, and——"

Druce looked up and smiled. "Why, of course,

I'd like to, very much." He held out his hand and Hamilton tossed him the keys.

"The larger one," Hamilton said, "is for the front door and the little one is for a drawer here in the desk. It's the lower one on the left—you can tell it because it's the only one that is ever locked."

Druce dangled the keys from his finger and looked up at his friend, interrogatively, as if he expected him to go on talking, but for a few moments there was silence, while Hamilton sat staring ahead of him, his brow wrinkled and his expression that of a man who was trying to reach a definite decision.

"Lloyd," he said at last, "if anything should happen to me—oh, I know," and he threw up his hand by way of protest—"of course nothing is going to happen—but I say if anything should happen, I wish you would come here and let yourself in and open the drawer that is locked and destroy anything you find there and—and don't waste any time about it."

Druce continued to twirl the key ring about his finger and then looked up suddenly and caught Hamilton's eye.

"Oh, I don't know, Wallie," he said, "it doesn't seem good enough to me. If you've got anything to destroy, why not do it now? You——"

"You don't understand," Hamilton interrupted.

"I know I don't understand. But I know that you, like every other man about to be married, are starting all over again—turning over a new leaf—not that the old one was damaged, at that. But for Heaven's sake, if you've got any closets with skeletons in them, now is the time to clean them out. At least, that's what I think."

Hamilton nodded and slowly rolled the end of his cigar between his lips.

"That's the trouble, Lloyd. That's what you think —that's pretty much what any one would think. Skeletons in my closets—bah! I never had any skeletons about me—I don't like them. I may have a decoration or two locked up, but no skeletons."

"What kind of a decoration?"

"Well, according to my ideas, there are all kinds of decorations. There are decorations of honor to the person who wins them as well as to the person who gives them, and there are decorations that re-

THE EXECUTORS

flect honor on the person who wears them and of dishonor on the one who awards them, and *vice versa*. Sometimes there is no tangible emblem—just a quarter of an hour—not that long, perhaps—but it's the quarter of an hour that means most in your life. There is nothing that can ever crowd out the memory of these decorations, and the worst of it is that to every one but yourself they are usually such foolish baubles—only tawdry pieces of junk that mean little or nothing—not even to the woman you are going to marry. And yet in our hearts we are forever turning back to them and the moment we won them. Do you suppose a man who won the Victoria Cross ever had the memory of that one brave act crowded out by any life of domestic happiness on the biggest estate in Great Britain? When I was a kid, I knew a boy who lived in a little town down on the Jersey coast, where I spent my summers, and he was the freshest, most unpopular boy in the village. He went to Princeton afterward and learned to race on one of those old-time high-wheeled bicycles. When he graduated, he went back to his native town and entered the mile bicycle race at the Spring Fair and licked the life

316

out of all of his old enemies. He afterward became
mayor of the town and bred the best race-horses in
the county and married a rich woman. But he told
me that often when the family had gone to bed he
used to get out the dinkey medal he won at the Fair
grounds and sit in front of the fire, and, by looking
into the flames, he could see the boys on the other
bicycles, with their matted hair and the sweat running
down their white cheeks, and he could see the banks
of faces of the crowd on either side of the track and
hear them curse him as he crossed the line. I knew
another man—about the best corporation lawyer
here in town to-day—he showed me once an old re-
volver that had been given him as a fee for his first
case in the town out West where he was born. His
client was a murderer and things looked altogether
hopeless, but my friend, the lawyer, made a wonderful speech, and the jury voted for acquittal. The murderer had no money, so he gave the lawyer the re-
volver he had killed the man with. That man's rich
and famous now; but when he showed me that old
gun, his eyes softened and he handled it as tenderly
as if it had been some living thing that had been

317

wounded. Whenever he looked at it, he said that his mind went back to the little, stuffy, crowded court-room out West and the lean, sorrowful looking face of the judge on the bench sitting all alone and the line of the twelve jurymen standing up, and at the end of the line the moon-faced foreman grasping the rail in front of him and saying 'not guilty.' That was *his* decoration; but what has it to do with the domestic life of the present great corporation lawyer? And yet, that was the best moment of his life. What do you suppose he would trade for that moment now?"

"I can't imagine," Druce said; "go ahead."

"And then," Hamilton continued, "there is another kind of decoration. Suppose a woman—I mean the one woman you remember when you are very ill, or when you have been in the open and away from civilization for a long time. Suppose just once that she had put her arms about you—I don't mean, necessarily, pink-and-white, well-rounded arms, with dimples at the elbow, but arms with nerves in them— nerves that not only go down to the heart but up to the brain too. Or, suppose a woman had never put her arms about you, but had just written you a line

318

of three words, 'I love you,' and suppose she had no right to write you that line, and the discovery of it would mean her finish, but she wrote it because it was the one real thing in her life, and because she wanted to show you that she trusted you. That's another kind of decoration—of honor or dishonor, whichever you choose to call it. You can't forget it, and I don't believe it's human nature to want to destroy the insignia that went with it, because that is always good for one real thri l."

Hamilton got up and walked over to the fireplace and looked down at his friend.

"I tell you, Lloyd, there are a whole lot of different kinds of decorations, and pretty much every man has one. You can't always see it because it may be at home in his desk, or it may be that there was no emblem that went with it; but believe me he knows it's there—hanging on his chest—not very far from his heart either."

Druce stretched his arms above his head and blew . a long cloud of gray smoke toward the ceiling. "All right," he said, "I'll keep the keys, but it's only because it's you."

Hamilton smiled. "It's only because you're you that I gave them to you."

Five days later, and two days before the date set for the marriage, a farmer driving a vegetable cart to town in the gray light of the early morning, found what there was left of Wallace Stillwell Hamilton and his racing car. The accident had taken place near Rye at the bottom of a steep hill, half way between the young man's own home and that of the girl he was so soon to have married. Hamilton was known as an occasionally careless, always fearless driver; the road had been rather slippery and the machinery of the car was demolished beyond the possibility of finding out the condition of the brakes at the time of the accident—that is, if it had occurred to any one to look at them, which, as a matter of fact, it probably had not.

Druce returned to town after the funeral, more genuinely depressed than he had ever felt before. Hamilton had been the best part of his life, and how much this friendship meant to him, how great was the void that no one else could fill, had begun to

320

strike home. He wandered aimlessly into his club, but whenever he came near, the men drew long faces, and their words of sympathy only hurt him the more; and so he went out again and walked slowly along those streets that seemed the least crowded. It was late in February, but the air was warm and damp and there was a heavy mist; the sidewalks were wet with melting snow, and the streets and gutters ran deep in mud and slush. With no heed as to where he was going, Druce walked aimlessly on, occasionally nodding back to faces that smiled and nodded to him. The mist turned to a light drizzle and a little later the drizzle to rain, and the warm drops blowing against his face brought him back to his surroundings. It was quite dark now and the street lamps were lighted and the sidewalks crowded with men and women going home from work. For a few more blocks he jostled along with the crowd, and then seeing an empty hansom pass, he hailed it and gave the driver the address of the apartment house where he lived. It was on his way there that he remembered the silver key ring and Hamilton's last request and his friend's injunction not to "waste any time about it." He found the keys at his rooms and set out for Hamilton's apartment at once, because he knew that the servant of his late friend was almost sure to be away at that hour and on this visit he wished to be alone and undisturbed. As a precaution Druce rang the bell, but as no one answered, he opened the front door and passed on into the sitting-room. He switched on the electric light and found that the shades of the windows which opened on the street were down and the curtains drawn. The air was damp and heavy with the odor of stale tobacco smoke, and the coal grate was half filled with gray cinders. It was evident that the room was just as its late master had left it. He closed the door, and walking very softly, as if afraid of disturbing the loneliness of the cheerless room, went over to the desk and sat down before it. For a moment he glanced about at the things on the desk he knew so very well—a small photograph of Helen Trask in a riding habit and a broad sailor hat, and a larger photograph of Hamilton's mother; the old-fashioned silver ink-well and the green leather rack filled with the familiar note-paper. On the broad blotter there lay a pen, just where Hamilton

322

had left it, and Druce hesitatingly picked it up and then quickly put it back just as he had found it.

The young man seemed to become suddenly conscious of the chill in the air, for the room was very cold, and he at once set about his task. He tried the little drawers of the desk until he had found the one that was locked, and then taking the keys from his pocket, inserted the smaller one in the lock. And, as he did so, he heard the rustle of a portière opening behind him, followed by a low cry, and turning he saw the mother of his friend and Helen Trask standing in the doorway. Unconsciously he rose to his feet, and at the same moment Mrs. Hamilton recognized him and came toward him.

"Oh, Lloyd," she said, "I'm so glad it's you. We had no idea any one would be here."

Druce put his arm about her, for she had always been much like a mother to him, and led her to a big arm-chair at the side of the desk.

"I'm afraid it's very cold for you," he said. "I'll try to start a fire."

He turned, and as he did so he saw Helen Trask standing before the desk, her eyes resting on the key ring dangling from the locked drawer. For a moment the girl's face, white and as expressionless as marble against her broad black veil, remained unmoved. Turning toward Druce she inclined her head very slightly, her colorless lips moved in words of an unheard greeting, and then her eyes turned back to the locked drawer.

He went over to the fireplace, but there was neither coal nor kindling of any kind.

"I'm sorry, Mrs. Hamilton," he said, "but I fear a fire is impossible. It's really very cold. Do you think you ought to stay?"

"It's only for a minute. Helen and I were so terribly lonely out there in the country that we thought we would come to town and spend the night with my sister. And then Helen wanted to come here—we thought the servant might be in, but the caretaker says he has not been back since—that is, for several days—and so he opened the door for us."

Helen sat down in the chair before the desk and turned her colorless face toward Druce. There was a certain questioning look in her eyes, which seemed to ask, even demand some sort of an explanation.

324

He walked over to the desk, and taking the key from the lock, dropped it into his coat pocket. Then he went back to his former stand before the fire.

"Mrs. Hamilton," he said, "I feel that I ought to explain why I am here. Some time ago Wallie told me if anything should ever happen to him that I should come here and look for some papers, in a particular drawer in his desk, and destroy them. I suppose they were some business papers—probably notes from people to whom he had loaned money which he did not wish ever to have collected. You know how Wallie was always doing something for people and never wanting to have it known?"

The mother smiled at him and nodded her head. "Why, of course," she said, "I've no doubt that's what it was. Wallie was so good to every one and he never spoke of his charities even to me."

Miss Trask was looking away from Druce, her elbows resting on the desk and her chin between her palms. "Did you say, Lloyd," she asked, "that it was long ago that he told you this? Before—before Wallie and I were engaged, I mean?"

"Oh, yes, long before. Probably a year or so ago."

"I can't understand that," the girl said without looking up, "because this is a new desk; I remember the day he got it; we all came here to supper that night. Don't you remember, it was not more than a month or so ago?"

The older woman looked up questioningly at Helen and then at Druce. After all, what difference could it make now—her boy was gone and a few papers more or less could not matter very much. For some moments there was silence and then it was Druce who spoke.

"You're quite right, Helen," he said. "He gave me the keys very recently. It was just the other night —the last time we were together."

The girl turned and looked at him. "And what are you going to do with these papers?" she asked.

"Destroy them—of course."

"Unopened?"

"Naturally—unopened."

For a moment the girl closed her eyes and brushed her forehead with the back of her gloved hand.

"I'm afraid," she said, "I don't quite understand.

Why should he ask you to destroy these papers?
Why should you try to deceive me about them?"

Druce clasped his hands behind his back and
looked the girl evenly in the eyes.

"I don't know that they are papers. All I know is
that he asked me to destroy something in that
drawer. I am simply trying to carry out the last
request of a friend. I do not believe that the papers,
if they are papers, are of any great value to any one
except to the man who left them."

"Value!" the girl repeated. "Has a name no value,
has a memory no value? Wallie Hamilton gave his
life to me—and I gave mine to him—and now all I
have left is that memory. I believed that it was a life
without blame, and that there was no secret he held
from me, and yet you would destroy that memory?
I am to go back to my grief with that suspicion
always before me? Do you think that it is fair to
throw up this barrier between his memory and my
love for him, which is the most real thing in my life?
You claim the rights of a friend—I claim the rights
of the life that he gave to me."

"Helen," Druce said, "you are making it very

hard for me. I only want to do my duty as I see it."

She rose from her seat at the desk, and going over to Mrs. Hamilton, sat at her feet and rested her head against her knee. The older woman gently brushed a loose strand of hair from the girl's eyes.

"I was his mother," she said, "his blood was my blood, and I am his legal executor. He was, I think, the best son a mother ever had, and yet no mother could know all of her son's life. My child, you are very young in the ways of the world and you are very tired, and you have suffered a great deal—more, I hope, than you will ever suffer again. I think you had better let me take you home."

The girl buried her head in the older woman's lap and cried softly to herself.

Druce turned away, and, resting his hands on the shelf over the fireplace, looked down on the cinders in the cold grate. For the first time he saw resting on the gray coals the charred remnants of a piece of paper—the fragile, twisted form in ashes of a burned letter—a breath would have blown it into a thousand flakes.

"Very well, Helen," he said, "I think it is better that you should have your way."

THE EXECUTORS

He went over to where the girl knelt and touched her gently on the shoulder. "Very well, Helen," he said, "I think it is better that you should have your way. You will probably find that the drawer is empty —he had no secret from you. Wallie always loved a joke."

He took the keys from his pocket and pressed them into the girl's hand. Then he bowed to the two women and went out and left them to their empty legacy.

When he had reached the street he stopped to look up at the familiar windows. On how many nights during the past few years had he glanced up at the same windows to see if the lights were still burning.

"Poor dear old Wallie," he said half aloud, still looking up at the dark, forbidding house-front. "Poor old Wallie—I did the best I could for you. And now that it's all over, I wonder who is the proper executor for a man's secret!"

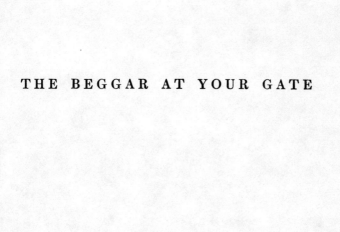

THE BEGGAR AT YOUR GATE

THE BEGGAR AT YOUR GATE

IT was one of those late afternoons in spring when the sky looks like a great turquoise and the air is filled with a wonderful golden haze. Switching a light bamboo stick, his eyes smiling from sheer good health, and his soul at peace, the young man swung from the gay, crowded avenue to the quiet of the side street. There was little chance at this hour that Arthur Keveney would be at home, but the fact that Keveney owned an automobile made the few steps easily worth the while.

But to the surprise and delight of young Latham, the elevator boy "believed" that Keveney was at home and Keveney's servant confirmed the suspicion. Latham found his friend stretched out in a deep chair before the open hearth, his feet resting on the brass fender.

The visitor leisurely laid his hat and cane on the table. "Hello, Arthur," he said, pulling at his gloves, "why so gloomy?"

Keveney continued to gaze moodily into the fire-less hearth. "Oh, is that you, Ned?" he asked.

"I've got a great idea, Arthur. Have you anything on for to-night?"

Keveney turned his foot on the fender and gazed at his silk-clad ankle bone with much the same interest that he would have regarded a piece of toasting bread.

"I don't know," he sighed. "I really don't know. I promised mother to go out to dine with her at Mamaroneck to-night, and that means that Helen Martin is coming to dinner, too."

Latham lit a cigarette and leaned against the mantel with his back to the fireplace so that he looked down on his friend.

"Sort of hard on the girl," he said. "Is that her only diversion?"

Keveney nodded. "It's bad enough for her to have to spend the winter in the country with a sick aunt, but to be brought over to our place in the hope that she and I will fly into each other's arms is a little too much."

"Such a nice girl, too," Latham said. "Why don't you?"

Keveney partially roused himself from his lethargy. "Why don't I marry Helen Martin? Because, in the first place, she probably wouldn't have me if I asked her, and in the second place, I don't want to marry anybody. If I wanted to marry, as a general proposition, I should certainly try to marry Helen Martin. She has beauty and brains and a great deal of charm and very few relatives—in fact, everything a wife should and should not have except money, and I've got all we need of that." Keveney pulled himself up to the edge of the chair and began a tirade to the fire-dogs. "But why should I marry? Look at these rooms—best bachelor apartment in New York. If I married I should have to have a whole house on the east side of Central Park and a big place in the country, and I'd have about one hundred servants to look after. Now, I have one man—and he's not a real man——"

"I think Simmons is a very good man," Latham interrupted.

"Of course, he's a good man—no better—but that's because he's not human, just a machine. I've had Simmons for years and I don't even know if he's

335

married. He may have a family of thirteen boys, for all I know. And that is another thing against marriage. Just think of the responsibility of children—picking out governesses and schools for them, and, when that's over, you've got to pick out colleges, and then you've got to pick out clubs and wives and husbands for them. That settles it—I will not dine with mother and Helen to-night. Why should I even run these chances? What was your idea?"

"My present idea is that you should go to Mamaroneck and take on a little responsibility."

Keveney shook his head. "No," he said, "absolutely no. What was your other idea?"

"My other idea," said Latham, proud of having done his duty and smiling with apparent pleasure at the thought, "is rather new. Quite a spirit of adventure about it Do you remember Paula Le Roy—show-girl for a time last winter at the Casino?"

Keveney nodded. "Even her name sounds like an adventure. What's the matter with Paula?"

"Vaudeville—going into vaudeville."

"Think of that! Isn't that a rather serious step for a pleasure-seeking blonde? She *was* blonde?"

Latham was becoming a little annoyed and showed it. "Certainly, she was and is blonde," he snapped, "and she is ambitious and wants to get out of the show-girl class. She has a very serious side to her."

Keveney sat back in his chair and resumed his former position of complete ease. "Ned," he asked, "did you ever call in a specialist for that trouble of seeing only the serious side of these butterflies of the stage? Really—it's growing on you."

Latham disregarded this last remark and with an unusual show of enthusiasm continued. "Now, vaudeville is not so easy as some people think. A girl has to get new songs, have them orchestrated, buy special clothes, hire a leader for a week or two until she gets easy, and then she has to find an engagement at some out-of-the-way place where she can try her act on for a week and where the managers can see her. Now, Paula Le Roy has got an engagement down at a little town on the end of Staten Island. She opens to-night, and I thought it would be rather good fun to run down and see her and then bring her back to supper. No?"

Keveney looked up at Latham, drew in his lips, and slowly shook his head.

"I've heard of men going to Borneo to search for an orchid, and I actually knew a chap who went to some hot alkali district out West to dig for the hind leg of a mastodon; but going to see a lady, a lady named Paula Le Roy at that, make her début in vaudeville on Staten Island has Peary, Nansen, the Duke of the Abruzzi, and all the other explorers beaten a mile. When do we start?"

It was well past eight o'clock when Keveney's glistening automobile drew up in front of the Palace Theatre, and the welcome accorded it by a throng of small boys and half-grown loafers was as sincere and boisteriously enthusiastic as the unique occasion demanded. Mrs. Springer, wife of the manager of the Palace Theatre, as well as its treasurer and ticket-seller, saw the approach of the automobile from afar and hurried from her glass box-office to the curbstone to welcome her guests from the metropolis. She was a stout, square-built woman, who wore gold-rimmed eye-glasses and smiled continually.

"Glad to see you, gentlemen," she puffed. "Miss Le Roy said you were coming. Walk in."

Keveney suggested paying for their admission, but the manager's wife only laughed at the idea and bowed them through the little door and past the old man who was taking tickets. The place had been built for a skating-rink, and, although fairly clean, was bare and very dismal looking, and the air was close and stuffy and ill-smelling. The narrow hall was crowded, and at the far end through the dim light the newcomers saw a small stage where moving pictures were being shown. Below the stage there was a man playing a piano.

"I've got to go back to my box-office," Mrs. Springer explained, "and sell tickets for a while. Will you come in with me, or will you watch the show and wait for Miss Le Roy's turn? Such a sweet, pretty thing she is, and a wonderful dresser—and to come all the way over to Staten Island to try on an act. It's too bad Adolph isn't here to look after you, but he's playing the piano for the moving pictures. There are seats reserved for you down in front."

Latham decided that he wanted to see the moving pictures and hear Adolph play the accompanying music, but Keveney accepted Mrs. Springer's invitation and followed her into the little box-office. While the manager's wife sold tickets to a few boys who had been waiting for her return the young man climbed up on a high stool and looked curiously about the walls at the ticket racks and the many signed photographs of past and present favorites of the vaudeville stage. The little line at the box-office window soon came to an abrupt end, and, with no more money in sight, Mrs. Springer turned to her guest and beamed on him through the gold-rimmed eye-glasses. "Not much of a theatre, I suppose you're thinking," she said.

Keveney raised his hand in protest.

"Oh, I know," the woman said. "Adolph and I worked on Broadway long before we came here. We didn't always live on Staten Island; no, indeed."

"But you like it?" Keveney asked.

The woman picked up a pack of stiff pasteboard tickets and let them run slowly through her pudgy fingers, so that they formed a little pile on the glass window-ledge. With her eyes still on the tickets, she smiled and nodded

"Yes, we like it—pretty well. It isn't just the life we were accustomed to, you know. Adolph was a piano-player for a music-publishing house and I used to compose a little—and play, too. I wrote 'Mated and Parted,' and 'Gone Astray.' Yes, I wrote 'em both—words and music. You didn't know that when I first met you, did you?"

Keveney shook his head.

Mrs. Springer shoved one of the pasteboard tickets through the little opening in the window and tossed a quarter into the money box. "But there is more money in this," she went on, still smiling. "It would be all right for Adolph and myself over there. The white lights and Broadway were good enough for us, but there are three kids growing up and they've got to be looked after, and then the air over here is much better for them."

"But you and your husband come to New York very often?" Keveney asked.

The woman shook her head reflectively. "Not so

often. You see it's something of a jaunt. There's the railroad to St. George and the long ferry ride and the trip uptown. It takes time, and we give two shows a day, and there's generally a rehearsal in the morning—and then it's hard to get help here, sometimes, so I often have to do the scrubbing. We try to keep the place clean. Go look for yourself." And Mrs. Springer smilingly pushed back the door that opened into the theatre. "Your friend will be missing you. Come out after the intermission and Adolph will take you back of the scenes. I want you to look us over thorough, and see what a good house-keeper I am."

Keveney joined Latham in the front row, and in a desultory way watched a lightning-sketch artist draw caricatures of public men on a blackboard, and as a finish to his act the artist did a drawing with color crayons of a lake scene in the mountains and labelled it "Moonlight." He was a middle-aged man, with a shiny frock coat which was very short and altogether too tight, and his trousers were too short, too, and bagged at the knees. When he had finished "Moonlight" he glanced down at the two well-dressed young

342

men in the front row and made a funny little formal bow to them in response to their applause, which was perhaps more vigorous than the picture seemed to deserve. After the lightning-sketch artist had disappeared from view, a sheet was lowered, and Elaine Audobon, a slight, hollow-cheeked girl, with short straw-colored hair and her waist decorated with a mass of cheap jewelry, took her place at the side of the stage and sang sentimental ballads, which were illustrated by highly colored pictures thrown on the sheet. Miss Audobon was followed by a Spanish dancer, who, clad in a very frayed and very soiled scarlet dress, stamped her red satin slippers and twisted and gyrated about the stage, which was all too small for the purpose. When the dance was over, Springer, the manager, arose from the piano, which was accepted by the audience as a sign that the first part of the performance was at an end.

Keveney and Latham followed the general exodus to the door, where they found Mrs. Springer and Adolph waiting for them.

"I'd like to take you back of the scenes," the manager said after the visitors had expressed their formal appreciation of the performance. "It'll strike you as funny after those Broadway theatres."

The young men found that this particular "behind the scenes" was a very small space divided from the rest of the hall by some cheap drapery thrown over a canvas partition; the stage was a platform of rough boards, and the only dressing-room, which was devoted to the women, was a flimsy affair made of scantling and reaching but half-way to the smoke-begrimed ceiling. Miss Paula Le Roy, looking particularly beautiful and regal and entirely out of place in an exquisite creation of lace and chiffon, topped by a wonderful hat of flamingo-pink tulle, stood as far apart from her fellow-artists as the limited space would permit. The Spanish dancer and the young blonde girl, who had sung the illustrated songs, had retired to the dressing-room, but the cartoonist stood leaning against the edge of the platform. At his side there was a short flight of broad steps leading to the stage and on these two women sat. One was young and pretty, with bright, smiling eyes, full lips, a well-rounded throat, and a plump, well-turned figure. The other was very much older, with a face that, in comparison to the young woman, seemed particularly hard, and yet the two were unmistakably sisters. The elder was dressed in the clothes of a boy. Over the thin, flat-chested, narrow-hipped figure she wore a black velvet coat and knickerbockers, black stockings, and low dancing shoes. The younger, and pretty one, was dressed as a girl in a low-cut bodice and short skirt of cheap yellow satin. At the appearance of Latham and Keveney the two women and the cartoonist stopped talking and the younger girl smoothed the short yellow skirt further over her knees. The space was so small that every one was within a few feet of every one else.

Miss Le Roy shook her head dismally at her friends and glanced at her gown of cobweb texture and then at the very rough surroundings. The ex-show-girl at once began an earnest whispered conversation with Latham, and Keveney followed the manager to the little group at the steps.

"Mr. Keveney—that's right, isn't it—Keveney?" Keveney bowed.

"I want you to shake hands with the Lazelle Sisters." The younger girl rose and held out her hand.

"This is Miss Mae Lazelle," and then the manager turned to the sister still sitting on the steps—"Miss Mettie Lazelle. Two splendid little dancers, as you'll see later. This is Mr. Marshall Doyle, the lightning-sketch artist you saw in the first part."

"What name, please?" the artist asked, putting his hand to his ear. "Didn't quite get it. Just a little trouble in this left ear."

"Keveney," the manager said, raising his voice—"Keveney."

The cartoonist nodded. "Good old name—any relation to the Keveneys of Yorkshire. I'm a Yorkshire man myself. My father often used to hunt with the Keveneys. I wasn't in this business always— bless your soul—no."

Miss Mae Lazelle glanced from the cartoonist to Keveney, and, with a smile of understanding, stifled a yawn.

It was not often the cartoonist met young men of the great world and so he hurried on. "You seemed to like that sketch, 'Moonlight.' I suppose I've drawn that picture a thousand times, but I thought I did it pretty well to-night—rather better than usual. I sold the original of that picture, in oil, for twenty pounds. Pretty good pay, eh?"

"Splendid!" Keveney answered. "I should think it would have paid you better to stick to oil."

The cartoonist scratched his chin and then slowly shook his head. "Too uncertain," he said; "all right when I was a young blade, but when you marry a woman used to all the luxuries in the world you must look for the sure money."

"Is your wife English, too?" Keveney asked, with polite interest.

"Indeed she is that—never been to America in her life."

The two women and Keveney looked up suddenly. For a moment the older woman, with pursed lips and smiling eyes, continued to stare at him. "And you support her over there?" she asked—"send her money?"

The man looked at the woman and then at the others in evident surprise. "Send her money? Of course I send her money—for twelve years and never a sight of her. But I married her, didn't I? I hold out ten dollars a week for myself—clothes is extra—and I send her the balance."

Mae Lazelle shook her pretty head and smiled broadly at Keveney and then at the cartoonist.

"You're a good thing," she said; "for sure, you're a good thing. '

The man nodded and shrugged his shoulders. "That's right," he said, "that's right. I'm a good thing as you say, but—but, well, I like it."

"Do you stop out here," Mettie Lazelle asked, "or do you go to town every night?"

"Oh, it's the big town for me," the artist chuckled. "There's always something doing there. It's a tough trip, but the only restaurant here is not up to the standard, eh? I saw you there after the matinée to-day."

Mettie Lazelle shook her head at the memory. "Did you try that mutton?" her sister asked. "It certainly had got by the age limit, all right."

Springer turned to Keveney and laughed. "These Broadway artists get awful particular when they play Staten Island. Will you come out in front? I'm going to beat the box again."

Keveney and Latham returned to their seats and watched another series of moving pictures, while Springer pounded out an *olla podrida* of marches, ragtime melodies, waltzes, and apparently anything that came into his head. Then with high, metallic voices the Lazelle sisters sang several coon songs, ending with an old-fashioned clog dance, and Miss Le Roy followed with what the programme announced as "the most refined musical act on the vaudeville stage." The object of their outing was over, and as there seemed to be no particular reason for the two young men to remain, they left their seats, and having paid their respects to Mrs. Springer in the box-office, went out to the sidewa k.

"Whew!" Latham sighed. "Wasn't it awful? And to think of breathing that kind of air twice a day, and all the year round, at that!"

Keveney nodded his head and drew a long breath of the pure fresh air into his lungs. "Awful!" he said. "It's bad enough to come over here in an automobile for one mad night, but just imagine those Lazelle girls making the trip to this forsaken village every day, rain or shine, and going back at night."

349

"And not going back to much at that, probably," Latham added.

"Springer told me that he gave thirty-five dollars for the pair of them, and you can't live very near the centre of the town for that—not New York town, anyhow."

The two young men climbed into the waiting automobile, lighted their cigars, and proceeded to make themselves as comfortable as possible until the arrival of Miss Le Roy.

It so happened that the ambitious show-girl and the Lazelle sisters left the stage-door at the same time, and as a result reached the sidewalk together. Miss Le Roy stopped for a moment to wish her sisters in art good-night, and Keveney and Latham got out of the car and joined the little group.

"Why not let us take you over?" Keveney suggested to Miss Mettie Lazelle. "I wish you would—there's lots of room for all of us."

The girl looked up at him as if she doubted that he was quite in earnest, and then smiled and held out her hand. Even if she had met few men like Keveney and Latham, she knew the type just as well

as she knew the Paula Le Roy type, and just as well
as she knew that there was nothing in common between their lives and the lives of a pair of hard-
working, underpaid girls who did a sister act in
cheap vaudeville houses.

"Thank you very much," she said, "but I think
we'd better run for the cars." The woman took her
sister's arm, and, nodding to the group, started to
go, but Keveney blocked the way. In the dull light
of the street lamps the younger woman looked even
fresher and prettier than she had when she was made
up for the stage, but the face of Mettie Lazelle was
drawn and the eyes looked tired and there were heavy
rings under them. From the bleached hair to the worn
shoes, the poverty of the woman's clothes as well as
her body seemed to cry out for sympathy. Keveney
turned to the younger woman.

"Won't you make your sister come?" he urged.

"Come on, Mettie," the girl said. "Don't pretend
you don't like automobiles just because you've never
been in one. A regular chauffeur could never find our
joint, but the gentlemen can drop us at the Subway.
Please let's go for a ride, Mettie."

THE BEGGAR AT YOUR GATE

A moment later Mettie Lazelle was reluctantly crowded into the back of the automobile, while Mae sat next to Keveney, who drove the car. To the boisterous farewells of Mrs. Springer the automobile shot out into the darkness, and the girl by Keveney's side clasped her gloveless hands, uttered a sigh, and settled back into the leather seat. "It's great, ain't it?" she whispered. "I always sort of knew I'd like it."

Keveney nodded and smiled at the pretty face. The night breeze had already brought a flush to the pale cheeks and was blowing little wisps of brown hair across the eyes grown big with excitement.

"I'll let her out," he said, "as soon as we get beyond the town."

"Sure," she said. "I'd like to go real fast—once."

In the distance they could see the lights of a train on its way to St. George. The girl raised her small, soiled hand and shook it at the passing cars. "Not to-night," she laughed, "not to-night."

"I should think that it would be much easier for you," Keveney said, "to live here rather than to take the trip over every day, especially as you have to come so early for the matinées."

The girl did not answer at once, but looked back at her sister, who was talking earnestly with Latham and Miss Le Roy.

"Yes," she said, "it would be better—a whole lot better. The boarding-houses aren't all bad in these small towns and it would save the travel at night—that's the fierce part of it. But Mettie has a flat in New York that she takes by the year, and so whenever we play in the neighborhood it's a good deal cheaper for us to run in."

"After all," Keveney said, "it's pretty good to have some place called home, isn't it?"

The girl glanced up at the young man and then out at the long shaft of white light before them. "Yes, I guess that's right," she said, and then, lowering her voice to almost a whisper: "Mettie got married when she was—oh, awful young, and she has a son—Gussie. He lives in New York and Mettie really keeps the place for him. It's more of a home for Gussie, you see, than Mettie and me. Of course, we're on the road a lot."

"I understand. How old is Gussie?"

"Gussie? Gussie's eighteen, I reckon, but then

353

he's the one man in the family, and of course being Mettie's only child——"

"How about the father?" Keveney interrupted.

The girl smiled. "Mettie's husband? He quit early in the game. He was a bad one, all right."

"I beg your pardon. I had no idea."

Miss Lazelle shrugged her shoulders. "Don't mention it. How could you have any idea? Mettie's all right. She has the kid and she hasn't time to worry over a husband. It takes all we can make to buy Gussie a home and cigarettes and keep him dressed up like a prince."

"I don't know much about the business," Keveney said, "but I should think that you could make more money in comic opera. No?"

"Meaning me?" and the girl pointed to herself, "or the team?"

"Why—you, I suppose."

Once more the girl glanced back at her sister, and then leaned over against Keveney. "Last spring, when we were working with a combination, I was offered fifty a week to go with a Chicago summer show. Fifty per for little Mae, would you believe it?"

"Fine!" Keveney said. "Didn't you take it?"

The girl looked up with wonder in her eyes.

"Take it?" she repeated. "Take it, and split the sketch and tell Mettie that she was a has-been—that her pipes were rusty and her shape was shrunk, and that her poor, dear face had too many ines worried into it? Tell her to go back to New York and sit in the flat and fold her hands and wait for remittances from the candy kid whom she taught everything she knows? No, Mr. Keveney, I didn't tell her that. Mettie and I are regular, not stage sisters. We went right on for thirty-five a week, and you can take my word for it, before I hand her the hook and take away her chance to work for Gussie, we'll be in a one-ring circus washing down the animal cages."

Keveney stirred uneasily in his seat. "Of course," he said, "I didn't quite grasp the real situation. I suppose I'm a little dull."

Once more the girl leaned over toward Keveney, brushed her shoulder against his, and turned her eyes on him in a glance that a mother might have vouchsafed a wayward child. The indignation had quite gone from her voice when she spoke again. "Don't you mind," she said consolingly, "if you are a little dull about a sister act. I'll bet there's lots of things you know that Mettie and I never heard of."

There was a sudden slowing down in the speed and the car swept across the open square in a long curve, and then rolled slowly down the gangway to the sheltered decks of the ferryboat. Keveney and the girl turned in their seats and listened to the conversation of the others in the back o° the car. Mettie Lazelle was te ling them of her experiences in some of the mining camps in which she and her sister had played, and of still earlier days when they had done a balancing act in a one-ring circus and sung in the "concert" after the show for an extra five dollars a week. She told them of how when Mae was only a child they had travelled in a wagon from one little town to another, taking a few hours' sleep whenever they could, and some days playing in barns and others in open lots, and how Mae passed the hat because she was so young and pretty; how the performance had frequently broken up in a riot, and how they had been stoned by the town hoodlums and often had to run for safety in their stage clothes.

356

The Lazelles smiled at these recollections of those stormy days which were even worse than the present, but Paula Le Roy and her two men friends could not quite see this humorous point of view. Perhaps it was that, in the indolence of their lives, they could not appreciate that the present estate of the Lazelle sisters was so much better than it had been in the days of the wagon-show. It was no more possible to listen to these stories of the early trials and the hardships than it was to look at the heavy shadows and the deep lines they had drawn on the bloodless, prematurely old face of the woman who told them and not have a wish to put out one's hand. But there was something in the manner of the Lazelle sisters, a certain rugged independence, a smiling indifference to the face of adversity that lifted them far above their surroundings, and to turn the thought of charity toward them into words would have been a simple rudeness. They seemed to belong to that small but very rich c ass who look only for the crevices in a wall that reaches across their path, and in a pigsty see nothing but the fugitive flower that has pushed its head through the muck to the clean air that is above it.

357

THE BEGGAR AT YOUR GATE

When they had reached the New York side and were on their way uptown, Keveney insisted that they should all go to his rooms, where he had ordered supper. Latham added his entreaties to those of his friend, but Miss Le Roy protested that her long trip and her first and arduous experience in vaudeville had made her fit only for bed, and Mettie Lazelle begged off on the excuse that her son would be waiting for her at home and that she could not give up one of the few opportunities she had of seeing him. With much reluctance Keveney dropped Miss Le Roy and Latham at their different apartments and then took the Misses Lazelle to their home far over on the West Side.

The home of the Lazelles was on one of those gloomy streets near the North River that are lined with old three-story brick dwellings and high, narrow apartment houses, the kind on which a great part of the money is spent on a fancifully trimmed façade and much brasswork about the doorway.

"I wish you would come in," the older Lazelle sister said. "It'll only be some beer and cheese sandwiches, but I'd like you to meet my boy, Gussie."

There seemed to be no adequate way for Keveney
to refuse, and so, although he was not sufficiently
hungry to enjoy cheese sandwiches, and although
beer did not agree with him at all, he accepted the
invitation with alacrity and an apparent display of
genuine pleasure.

The janitor had forgotten to light the hall lights,
or perhaps they had been turned out for the night,
but, in any case, Miss Lazelle gave the young man
her hand, and the trio, laughing as they went, stumbled up four flights of narrow stairs, and, with the
help of Keveney's matches, opened the front door
of the Lazelle flat.

"Gussie's probably tired and fallen asleep," Mettie Lazelle explained to Keveney, as she led him to
the sitting-room at the end of the narrow hallway.
But Gussie was nowhere to be seen, and the two
women went into their bedroom to take off their hats
and for the moment left Keveney alone in his new
surroundings. The sitting-room was very small and
the air was close and had the damp smell peculiar
to all over-crowded, ill-kept apartment houses. A few
colored prints of women's heads in gold frames hung

against a wall-paper of yellow and scarlet roses. There were no globes to shade the lights from the four blazing gas-jets of the chandelier, and the glare threw into a sharper relief the contrast between the crude color of the new wall-paper and the faded rep curtains, the frayed green covers of the cheap furniture, and the well-worn carpet. On the mantel-shelf and standing in frames on the centre table were many photographs in costumes of the Lazelle sisters and their friends of the vaudeville stage. Keveney having made a tour of the room sat on a lounge, which was evidently used as a bed by night. Mettie came in patting the straw-colored wisps of hair over her forehead, and sat in a rocking-chair at the centre table directly under the blaze of yellow light. The sister followed a few minutes later and curled herself up on the far end of the lounge. There was a conspicuous silence while Mettie folded her hands and looked anxiously at the nickel alarm clock on the mantel. For the moment there seemed to be no particular topic of general interest.

"I'm sorry about Gussie," Mettie said at last. "You see, he runs around the corner to Regan's for the supper after we get in—the beer is fresher that way and they make the sandwiches up new for him. I'd like to have you meet Gussie, too."

"I'm very sorry," Keveney said as impressively as he could. "Your sister tells me that your son lives in town. I suppose he is in business here?" Mettie looked up again at the clock, pursed her thin, colorless lips, and shook her head.

"No," she said, "Gussie isn't in business here— that is, not just now: Gussie seems to have hard luck. I guess they probably don't understand the boy. He had a good job for a while as checker in a department store and he worked on the delivery wagons for a time, but business was bad and they laid off a good many, and of course, Gussie being new—and then he was usher for a while down at Miner's Theatre, but I was glad when he quit that. There wasn't much money in it and I'd rather keep him away from show business. I suppose you think it's better for a boy to work though, don't you?"

Keveney nodded.

"Yes, of course," the woman went on dully. "I guess that's right; keeps them off the street and away

from the pool-rooms and such places. I don't suppose
you know of anything in your line of work. Now,
if—" The woman's dull eyes suddenly brightened
at the thought and she looked up eagerly at her guest.

"Why, Mettie," the younger sister interrupted.
"You oughtn't to ask Mr. Keveney that. We got
no right to ask him any favors."

The light faded from the woman's eyes as quickly
as it had come, and raising both hands to her scrawny
neck, she put her fingers between the collar of her shirt-
waist and her throat, as if the linen band was chok-
ing her. "That's right," she said slowly; "I beg your
pardon. I didn't think, but Gussie's such a fine boy."

There was a slow shuffle of feet in the hallway; a
young man with a brown derby hat pushed far back
over his forehead and a dead cigarette hanging from
his lips stood swaying in the doorway. He was very
thin and anæmic-looking, with tow-colored hair and
weak, watery blue eyes, and colorless lips and cheeks.
The younger sister sat on the lounge, gazing steadily
at the newcomer; Mettie Lazelle walked to his side
and tried to put her arms about his shoulders, but the
young man pushed her away.

"That's all right," he said.

Mettie turned to Keveney. "This is my boy, Gussie. Gussie, this is a friend of ours, who brought us over from Staten Island—Mr. Keveney."

The young man took off his hat and moved unsteadily toward him. "Glad to know you," he said, and held out a thin, trembling hand.

"Gussie," Mettie suggested, "we thought you would go for some beer. We promised Mr. Keveney some."

"Sure," the boy muttered, "some beer and sandwiches," and turned again toward the door.

As he did so, Keveney rose too, and, protesting that it was too late to stay longer, bade his hosts good-night. The two women accompanied him to the hall doorway and he left them standing there with their arms about each other's shoulders, and slowly followed the boy down the dark stairways.

When they had reached the sidewalk Keveney said good-night and perfunctorily put out his hand, but Gussie seized and held it in a tight grasp. "Glad to know you," he said. "Come in and see us often.

Nice girls, Mother and Mae—nice girls. Is that your machine?"

Keveney nodded and tried to release his hand, but the young man refused to let him go. "Sorry to trouble you on short acquaintance," he stammered, "but I'm in a sort of difficulty. Went to the track this afternoon and lost every cent Mother gave me to pay the rent with. Don't suppose you can let me have a loan of twenty?"

Keveney wrenched his hand loose and took a twenty-dollar bill from the roll of money in his pocket and gave it to his new acquaintance.

"That's for the rent, you understand," he said, "not to play the races, and don't think I'm doing it for you. It's for your mother and aunt."

The young man swayed slowly and looked down at the bill, which he held tightly between his hands. "I'm certainly obliged," he muttered. "You're all right, young fellow; you're all right."

Half an hour later, when Keveney got back to his apartments, he found Simmons patiently waiting for the supper party.

"I'm alone, Simmons," he said, "but I'm hungry. Give me whatever you have ready."

Keveney went into the big sitting-room, where the servant had arranged the table. There was a luxurious warmth in the mellow colors of the very room itself that made the young man rub his hands together and smile. He glanced at the white table with a great bunch of jonquils in the centre; at the heavy, glistening silver, the gold-traced china, and the long-stemmed Venetian glasses reflecting a thousand colors in the orange glow from the shaded candelabra. And then, although he had left it but a few hours before, he walked slowly about the room, smiling at the pictures, the sideboard, with its row of shining silver racing trophies, the pieces of bric-a-brac he liked the best, and at the big comfortable leather chairs. He noticed how his feet sank into the heavy rug, and even the fireless hearth, with its burnished fire-dogs, looked warm and grateful. It was as if he were coming home after a long journey to a strange land and strange people. And then Simmons came in and the young man sat down to his lonely supper. He took a sip of champagne from one of the long-stemmed glasses, and then, smiling, looked up at the inscrutable face of Simmons, who was standing at the far end of the table.

"That tastes very good, Simmons," he said; "very good."

The servant, suddenly startled into life, acquiesced in a low and respectful bow.

"It tastes particularly good Simmons," Keveney exclaimed, "because I came very near having to drink beer and eat cheese sandwiches."

The servant again bowed and cast a hurried glance of alarm at his master.

Keveney picked out a cherry from the grapefruit before him and then held the long-stemmed glass before the light from the candelabra, and gazed reflectively at the air bubbles chasing one another to the top of the yellow liquid.

"Beer and sandwiches, from Regan's," he said. "I don't believe Simmons, you know where Regan's is."

The servant shook his head in much confusion. "No, sir," he said, "I do not, sir."

In a long term of service Simmons had never before heard his young master so loquacious, and the novelty of the situation was rather embarrassing.

"Simmons," Keveney continued, "there are a whole lot of folks and places you and I have never heard of. I've been on a long voyage and I met a great many wonderful people. There was a man and his wife who are marooned a thousand miles from here on a mud flat at the end of Staten Island. They have a little theatre there, set down among a lot of hovels, and although they love the lights of Broadway, they work and work and work for three children that are growing up."

"Yes, sir," Simmons said. "Will you have the asparagus with you chicken, or afterward?"

"At the same time," Keveney answered. When the chicken and asparagus were before him, and Simmons had again taken his plastic stand at the head of the table, Keveney continued to describe his wanderings in strange lands:

"And there was a deaf man who drew pictures— very bad pictures—and he had drawn bad pictures for tweve years so that he could send money to a wife that did not care enough to visit him in all that time. There were two women, too, who danced and sang and starved themselves, and all for a young man who would much better be dead. The older of them worked and starved because the young man was her son, and the young girl worked and starved because the older woman was her sister."

Keveney stopped talking and broke a roll in two, then tossed both pieces back on the table.

"Simmons," he said, "are you married?"

The servant nervously rested both of his hands on the back of the chair at the head of the table.

"Yes, sir. ·I've been married nearly fourteen years."

"Really," Keveney said. "That's a long time—fourteen years. Any children?"

"Yes—one, sir. A girl."

"That's very nice. I suppose she goes to school?"

The servant's fingers tightened perceptibly on the back of the chair.

"No, sir; she doesn't go to school. She's not very well, sir."

Keveney looked up from his plate to the man's face—no longer a mask, but the real face of a real man, with a heart and soul looking out through human eyes. For some moments there was silence.

"That's too bad," Keveney said at last—"too bad. Has she—I suppose she has everything?"

"Everything we could do. The missus is a wonderful nurse. Will you have your coffee now, sir?"

"No, thank you. I don't want any coffee. Get me a cigarette."

The young man lighted the cigarette and pushed his chair back from the table and crossed his legs.

"I suppose you mean," he said, "that your daughter needs things you and—and the missus—can't do for her?"

The servant nodded. "Not that you haven't been more than generous, sir, but those specialist doctors and operations——"

"Of course," Keveney interrupted. "That will be all for to-night. I'll put out the lights."

When Simmons had reached the door he turned back toward the young man. "Nothing more, sir?"

"Nothing more," Keveney said. "Except I wish you would call up my doctor in the morning—you know, Doctor Emerson—and make an appointment

for your little girl. I don't know whether he is ihe
kind of doctor you want, but he'll put you right.
Give him my regards, will you, and tell him to go as
far as he likes? Good-night."